STARFIRE

BOOK ONE OF THE STARFIRE WARS

JENETTA PENNER

STARFIRE

ISBN: 9781983319990

Printed in the USA

First printing 2018

CHAPTER 1

My father named me after the stars. But I've always preferred to keep my feet on the ground.

Ironically, I'm hurtling through space in a gigantic starship twenty thousand light-years from Earth. The only life I've ever known was there—school, my friends . . . Mom. This journey was Mom and Dad's dream, not mine, and she's the one we left behind.

I fumble for the simple gold band encircling my right ring finger and twist it. Now all I have left of her after she died is this piece of jewelry.

I'd rather have her.

The muscles in my stomach tighten and I exhale loudly. I glance at a glass computer panel, which displays a glowing image of Arcadia—the new Earth—our destination. The planet pretty much looks like old Earth but the continents are all mixed up, and it boasts two moons. The planet's atmosphere also glows a strange shade of cyan. On the occasional night, the atmosphere creates amazing patterns like the aurora borealis. Or so I'm told. The planet is uninhabited except for wildlife.

Ten years ago my mom, Isabel Foster, discovered how the atmosphere was similar to Earth's. My parents had worked tirelessly alongside the World Senate to streamline Arcadia's settlement and were told, repeatedly, that the process would take a minimum of fifty years before the first permanent international colony would set foot onto a new planet. Yet we'll temporarily disembark at the Skybase orbiting above Arcadia in less than eight hours.

Arcadia is a perfect Earth 2.0—ripe for the picking. I sigh while twisting the ring on my finger once again. Theory had always claimed that humans would need to make an inhospitable environment capable of supporting human life by completely restructuring a planet through terraforming. But this planet was just dangling out in space, waiting for us. And here we are. This discovery shifted Dad's plans for Arcadia to an urban development focus since it was considered an Easily Terraformable Planet.

Most days, Dad remains excited, but without Mom here, his moods are typically mixed. Though since our starship voyaged out of the Turner Space Fold, I've barely seen him, so I wouldn't know his mood today. To ensure safety, the captain of our starship, *Pathfinder*, had programmed our exit point for a seven-day lightspeed journey to the new Earth. Since then, Dad has been too busy making all the preparations and meeting with people I've never met or don't care about. I guess when you're the man who envisioned every aspect of how humans plan to live on Arcadia, people seem to think you're important or something.

His importance is evident by the cabin we were assigned, which consists of two good-sized rooms plus a small office for Dad. There's even a living room and a little eat-in kitchen with a set of barstools at the counter. The refrigerator is stocked with food, and if the supplies start to dwindle, a cute delivery guy shows up to replace the missing items.

Most of the people down below are lucky to receive a bunk and a nutritional food pack for the day. Ninety percent of these individuals probably felt like they had won a lottery ticket to the planet when they came out on top of their job testing. But the privilege also entitles them to a lifetime of indentured servitude on our new "Eden." I doubt many will ever repay the debt incurred just from the ticket price alone. Arcadia needs ready workers, however, and most had lived in slums and were starving while on Earth, so maybe being indentured was a better option.

The remaining voyagers bought their way onboard. They're the types who typically have piles of money to spend and were no doubt bored with Earth. Coming to a new world was hyped up as the chance of a lifetime, and if you have the cash to blow, why not blow it on building a new colony?

Princes and paupers. Not many passengers in-between.

I return my attention to my Earthscape lesson. Apparently, in my distraction, my entire simulated society has suffocated from a lack of oxygen in their domed city. Poor planning on my part. I sigh and tap off the program. When both of your parents specialized in terraforming and urban development, the expectation is that you'll do the same, especially when you began to understand the concepts before you were five. I do have a knack but not the passion—when I want to focus, that is. I'm only seventeen; why am I required to know what I'm going to do with the rest of my life? Maybe I want to be a painter. Don't need to travel across the galaxy to make that dream a reality. Mom never pushed me to make important life choices before I was ready.

I stand, brushing my wavy, strawberry blond hair off my forehead, and go over to the nightstand beside my twin bed to search for a clip. Mom's jewelry-making tools—colorful beads and glistening gems and an array of metal fasteners—cover the surface. She was in the middle of teaching me her hobby when . . . when we ran out of time. We did fashion a few pieces together, though, and I even managed to partially cobble together a ruby tie tack on my own. After it's done, I plan to give it to Dad when we reach Arcadia. I might not be excited, but he is, and I love him.

I pick up a sapphire clip Mom made and affix it to the right side of my hair. Then I grab my green sweater hanging across the chair's back and run my arms through the sleeves. This particular shade of green—a deep emerald—not only matches my eyes, it's also my favorite color. Fashion and matching eye color aside, there's an odd draft that always seems to be present in the corridors. I'm not sure the mystery breeze is a good thing, but the colonization site on Arcadia tends to lean toward tropical. I'll never be cold again.

Exiting my room, I amble through the silence of our unit. Once I enter the living area, I stop momentarily to stare at the blur of stars outside of our window. The blackness streaked with white light made by our forward motion takes me farther away from Mom and everything I left behind. With a gulp, I resume my pace to the door and tap my hand on the release. The door whooshes back and reveals a brightly lit hall.

I step out of the unit and glance behind at the bronze placard on our door:

Richard Foster
Cassiopeia Foster

The names are listed as if we are movie stars or something. It's weird. No one else on our wing has names on their doors, only unit numbers. Maybe the other members of the Board do too. But I have not been to their units. I shake my head and veer to my left toward Dad's dedicated workspace. Maybe he has a few minutes for us to grab lunch and talk about tonight's gala planned for after our Skybase arrival. The party is a good distraction, and I'm sure he needs a break too.

Halfway there, I check the time on my Connect: 11:17 a.m. I exhale in frustration. I know Dad. He'll be engrossed in a project until closer to noon. My best odds for pulling him away are to waste the next twenty-five minutes. So, I take a right toward the arboretum wing. The space is quiet, and the crowded plants spark memories of family trips we used to take to visit Grandma, who lived out in the country.

The five-minute stroll and elevator ride a few floors up are worth every second spent. My shoulders relax a notch as I stroll through the gigantic, nearly park-like setting. I scan the space for any other people, but there's no one. It seems like everyone else is working all the time. Looking up, I watch as simulated white, puffy clouds float across an equally simulated blue sky. Around me, buzzing worker drones called Agrowbots—roughly the size of pigeons—tend to trees heavily laden with fruits of all kinds. The bots pollinate, prune, and dispose of dead leaves and any overripe produce. If I squint hard at their white, pearly bodies, I can pretend that the bots are real birds, as if I'm outside instead of inside an artificial arboretum. Even the soothing sounds of a rolling breeze and the chirping insects are fake. Not as if the pigeon drones would allow any insects into their perfect orchard.

I approach a tree and reach for a blushing apple. With an easy snap, I pluck the fruit from the tree limb. I rotate the apple in my hands and study the impeccable skin before biting into the crispy flesh. Tart and sweet, the juice floods my taste buds. Pink Lady, my favorite. I grab a second and tuck it into the pocket of my sweater for Dad. They're his favorite too.

I take my time perusing the trees and manicured gardens, hard-pressed to spot one blemish. But with the lack of foot traffic, I'm not even sure why the ship is equipped with an arboretum. Our journey is only one week and everyone is working eighteen-hour shifts. Work, eat, sleep. Rinse and repeat. No time for nature.

Sighing, I toss the skeletal core to the ground. The second it hits the grass, a drone buzzes in and gobbles the apple into its belly's trash compartment, where the organic components will break down into usable compost. In real life, I'd never litter. But it's entertaining to watch the hungry pigeons. Even if the bots are not real birds.

I glance at my Connect again. The clear device accomplishes quite a bit for a small piece of tech. If I tap the face, an interactive holograph will appear that I can use to relay communication, or as a computer. But mostly, I use the device as a watch. 11:38 a.m. Close enough. It will take me a few minutes to get to Dad, anyway.

I exit the arboretum and pass a few unfamiliar, busy-looking faces along my way to meet Dad. Everyone holds such a serious expression. You'd think there would be more excitement. I hope once we arrive at Arcadia, people receive much-needed down time to enjoy their new lives. But I have a feeling none of that will happen.

I chew the inside of my lip as the elevator rolls up, releasing my lip when the doors slide open at deck twenty-five. From my vantage point, I spot Dad wearing a tan jacket and hustling down the corridor and away from me. He always complains about the mysterious draft on the ship too. Even though no one else seems to notice the breeze. I open my mouth to call out to him and then quickly snap my lips shut, realizing he's too far away and I would need to yell to get his attention. Shouting is something the snooty people in charge look down on around here. As I step out of the elevator, my father makes a left down a wing I haven't visited. Then a group of his team members come into view and follow him.

I tap my Connect and bring up a hologram of his itinerary. No, he doesn't have a conference scheduled until 3:00 p.m. And Dad is a stickler for schedules.

My stomach grumbles, ready for a more significant meal than an apple. I glance around for any signs the wing is off-limits, but there are none. So, I head in the direction he took. I turn the corner just as the last of the group behind him files into an unmarked conference room. As the door slides shut, I hear Dad's angry voice rumble through a nearby wall. Just my luck, he *is* in there.

Defeated, I decide to retreat and spend lunch in solitude. Typical. But the door makes a scraping sound on the track and then grunts when it sticks about a half-inch open. Once more, Dad's voice, thick with negative energy, pipes out from the narrow opening. Grumbles from voices I don't recognize step over whatever he's saying.

I shrug and peer around again. No one is here and I've got nothing better to do, so I might as well be a little bit nosy. What can the Board do to me? I'll just confess I was here for lunch and searching for my father. Which is true. A slap on the wrist is the worst they'd dole out.

I creep toward the door and position my ear as close as I can without being noticed. As an only child growing up, I had many opportunities to sneak around and listen to grown-up conversations that I wasn't really supposed to hear. I always felt guilty, but I never could stand being out of the loop.

"You can't let *her* get away with it," Dad pleads.

Several voices meld together through the crack in the door, and I lean my ear in closer to discover just who *her* might be and what exactly it is *she* can't get away with.

The clop of heavy boots on flooring echoes from around the corner and my breath hitches. Luckily, ten feet away, a short hallway connects a group of offices. On my toes, I dash for the hall's safety. Just as I round the corner, a woman's frame comes into view.

I let out a breath, knowing she didn't see me, and then squat to peek from my hiding spot.

Oh—*her*. Elizabeth Hammond. Mid-sixties, dyed white blond hair, and a scowl as a permanent accessory. The President of the Board . . . and my Dad's archenemy. I should've known from the disdain in his voice. The woman has spent her career mostly objecting to my father's ideas. He's always had innovative concepts, and the Board is conservative, especially Hammond. She's a rule follower to the core.

Oil and water.

She slams her hand to activate the door and it slides back with a scrape. I grit my teeth at the sound and the hairs on the base of my neck stand on end. Hammond doesn't flinch. And instead of entering, she stands in the opening. The conversation inside goes silent.

"Dr. Foster, I am unclear as to why I was not invited to this meeting," Hammond says, her voice thick with venom. No one breathes a word.

"President Hammond," Dad finally speaks up.

His voice is strong, but I know him well enough to pick out a tinge of fear. He's using the same tone as when he had told me a year ago that Mom had been killed in a vehicle accident. I'll never forget every minute detail of the moment I heard him say that Mom would never be coming home again. An ache blooms in my chest, and for several beats of my heart, I forget how to breathe. Too much. It's just too much to think about. Too incomprehensible. In that moment a year ago, I stuffed the feelings away as much as I could. Then something simple like the tone of a voice rushes fresh pain to the present. I gnaw on the inside of my lip and force myself to focus on the brewing argument just feet away.

"You are not unaware of our . . . difference of opinion on this issue," Dad continues. "And by the expression on your face, I get the impression that inviting you here would've been fruitless."

My pulse races in my ears. Everything in me wants to run to my dad and tell him everything is going to be okay. But doing that would get us both in trouble.

Hammond crosses her arms over her chest and throws her weight to her right side. "Then it's fruitless for you to call the meeting in the first place. No decisions are made without my consent."

"But my team has information I hadn't even considered," he says. "I needed to hear them out and compile the data. Any repercussions will emerge on the Earthscape program. When you see it, you might change your mind."

"I don't need the data," Hammond practically growls. "I've seen all I require to make the best choice for the people." With those words she spins toward the door and marches out with weighty boot steps.

Before the door scrapes shut, I hear my father sigh. "Not *all* of the people."

CHAPTER 2

I smooth out the skirt's pale-pink silk on the full-length formal dress I chose for tonight's Arrival Gala. In only a short while, we'll drop out of lightspeed and Arcadia will come into view. I'm sure there'll be plenty of "oohs" and "aahs" from the partygoers, but I've pretty much stared at Arcadia every day for the last ten years. I know this planet like the back of my hand.

I glimpse at myself in the mirror fastened to my bedroom's door. Tilting my head, I push away a fallen tendril of hair, loosened from a very amateur chignon over my left ear. Mom was always better at hair than I am. My lips dip into a frown and I swallow back the familiar ache.

"This will have to do," I mumble, and then I adjust the thin dress straps on my shoulders. Everyone will be watching Dad anyway unless I do something stupid, like slurp my soup too loudly or take a tumble down the stairs.

A tumble? Perfect reason to wear flats instead of pumps. Much safer. I spot the silver pair of ballerina flats in my closet, grab the shoes, and shove my feet in.

Outside my room, I hear Dad groan a few curses. The sound makes my stomach clench. He only swears when he's under extreme stress. Whatever happened today with President Hammond, plus Mom's absence, must be weighing heavily on his heart. And there's little I can do about it.

No. I *can* do *something*. I reach for a small box I had wrapped in a red bow. I didn't get to enjoy lunch with Dad today, so I spent the afternoon completing the tie tack for him.

Clutching the gift in my hand, I exit my room.

"Dad? Everything okay?" I call out.

"Uh . . . fine," he answers from the living room. I smile at the familiar sound of his deep voice, one I've always thought was kind. "I just can't get this tie knotted right."

As I walk into the living room, our eyes connect in the mirror hanging over the sofa as he stares at his reflection. Unable to stop myself, I chuckle. One end of his tie hangs down about six inches too far and the other end is six inches too short.

"Let me help you," I say as I lay my gift on the side table. I'm not good with hair, but I can knot a tie.

"Thanks, sweetie. Where would I be without you?" Dad says, wearing a sheepish look on his face as he unwraps the tie from around his neck.

"Where would we be without each other?" I say as I take the strip of blue fabric from his hand. "We're a team."

Dad smiles and his green eyes twinkle. His eye color is about the only physical feature I inherited from him; everything else was from Mom's DNA. He's six foot two. I'm barely five foot four. And before his hair went nearly gray, the color was chocolate brown, unlike Mom's and my strawberry blond tresses.

"Team Foster," he says.

"Forever. Now hold still so I can do this right."

He obeys, allowing me to run the tie around his neck. I make quick work of my specialty, a Windsor Knot. When I'm done, he checks himself in the mirror and straightens his charcoal-gray suit coat.

"There now," I say and look him over. "Almost ready."

He peers down at himself. "Almost? I don't think I can handle much more."

I smile and grab my red-bowed package. "I have a gift for you."

"A gift? I saw you brought me an apple from the arboretum. You know I love Pink Ladies."

"Not that." I hold out the box. "Open it."

He takes it, slowly unties the red ribbon, and then removes the paper. Before he opens the lid, his lips pull into a smile. "You didn't have to get me a gift."

"Dad," I scoff. "The last ten years of your life is being realized tonight. Arrival is an important occasion."

"But it's not as if *you* want to be here."

"Well, I am." I smile. "Now open it."

He pries open the top and reveals the bright ruby tie tack inside. "Wow," he says, grinning from ear to ear. But as quickly as the smile had come, it drops from his face, and then he turns and plops onto the sofa.

My heart plummets into my stomach. "You don't like it?"

Dad rubs his free hand over his face. "I love it. But tonight isn't what I intended it to be."

"You mean Mom?" I carefully sit next to him and straighten my skirt. My heart aches for her to be here with us too.

He nods. "Yes, but there's so much more."

He's referring to the horrible conference this afternoon, but I can't breathe a word I know about it.

Dad straightens and looks me in the eyes. "Cassi, if I teach you one thing—always follow your principles.

"You know I do."

"Yes, yes," he says. "But there are times when no one will understand your reasoning. And you'll need to find a way to hold your ground."

"What do you mea—"

Before I get the chance to finish, he taps his Connect. "Oh . . . the time is getting away. We need to go." He grabs the tie tack from the box and pins it on. "Look okay?"

"Yeah, Dad," I say, still full of concern and confusion.

He pops up from the couch and gestures me to the door. "It won't look good if we miss the unveiling."

As soon as we enter the glistening Gala hall, the on-location management team immediately descends on us. The staff members are dressed in black to blend into the background when their services are not needed anymore. Two men and one woman, with comms in their ears and tablets in hand, escort my father out of sight and to his designated place for our Skybase arrival.

Of course, the workers don't care about me outside of duty. A glove-clad staff member supplies me with a sparkly drink called a Grape Galaxy.

"Take a sip," the lady wearing a tight bun says.

Like a good girl, I smile and sip the dark purple beverage. The thing is overly sweet and fizz shoots up my nose. But I nod at her and hold my hand in the air, indicating that I'm fine, so maybe she'll go away.

"Have a good time, honey," she says and then leaves me to my own devices.

As I watch her buzz off like a worker bee, I run my free hand over my arms. The prickly hairs stand on end. In our excitement to leave, Dad and I forgot our coats. The winter temperatures that someone is fond of keeping in this ship are more extreme than ever tonight. Yet if I try and slip out to return to my unit, a worker dressed in black will only drag me back here, saying the unveiling will happen soon. I drop the mostly undrunk drink on a tray belonging to the first server who passes by.

Unfamiliar, fancily dressed adults sip drinks all around me. Drinks with sillier names than Grape Galaxy that I'm sure, unlike mine, are full of more than juice and seltzer water. Everyone seems to have a lot fewer concerns than I do, laughing and speaking way too loudly, probably from the alcohol. Or maybe the patrons really just don't have any worries. Human and bot servers both attend to their every need and circulate the room with trays of exotic finger foods. Gigantic floor-to-ceiling windows line the space, but the curtains are all closed in anticipation of the big reveal. The only stars we see are the twinkling lights from multiple crystal chandeliers.

I wind my way through the jungle of tables, towering floral centerpieces, and partygoers. Finally, I spot my place card on a table and walk toward my seat, relieved. At least if I sit, I can grab a roll from the basket without anyone noticing. I can nearly taste the crusty French bread smeared in butter—

"Cassiopeia Foster," a deep voice says from behind, drowning out the chatter and ruining my chances at a roll. "I was hoping to run into you."

Disappointed, I spin around to see who's calling me. It's not like I really know anyone on the ship except Dad and few of his associates. A tall boy, almost a man really—since I'm pretty sure he's older than I am—stands about five feet away. His wavy brown hair falls over his forehead and casually across his left eye, though I can still see shades of blue peeking through the strands.

"Do I know you?" I ask, fully aware I've never seen him in my life.

He struts toward me, hand extended. "No, we haven't met *yet*. I'm Luca Powell."

I smile sweetly and assume the role I'm here to play tonight: supportive daughter of Richard Foster. Without hesitating, I take his hand and give it a firm shake and look him in the eye.

He grins and releases my grip. "Confidence. I like that."

"My father taught me well."

"I'm sure he did," he says as he stares at me.

I cross my arms over my chest, not sure of what to do with my hands from the utter lack of pockets in my formal gown. "So, Mr. Powell," I say and glance around at the other patrons. "You're a bit younger than the rest of the crowd. What are you doing at the Gala?"

He chuckles. "I know what you're thinking. I must be some rich guy's son who bought his way into the party."

"The thought did cross my mind."

Luca puffs up slightly. "Well, you'd be wrong. My family didn't even come here with me and I worked my way into this position. You're staring at the newly inducted assistant to President Hammond."

My throat tenses. Hammond? If he's Hammond's assistant, this guy must know about the rift between her and my dad. Maybe she sent him to be *friendly* just to get information on me. Especially after this morning.

"Oh?" is all that comes out of my mouth.

"Yeah." He leans in close, smelling of spicy cologne. My nose tickles worse than it did from the fizzy Grape

Galaxy. "I was thinking, since your father is high-ranking and I'll be taking on more responsibility when we reach Arcadia, you and I should be friends."

Hammond definitely sent him to spy on me, or maybe even to keep me in line.

"I . . . I'm sure you're going to be very busy. Too busy for someone like me." My mind spins with possible ways to make an exit, but none of my ideas end in success.

"Ms. Foster?" a new male voice comes from my left.

"Yes?" I say, a little too quickly. Another boy my age, dressed in black attire like the crew, a color now representing my salvation. He's shorter than Luca with spiky, dark blond hair and gray eyes. I know nothing about him, either. But I'm pretty sure he's not another one of Hammond's assistants, so I already like him better.

"We're about to arrive and I've been requested to escort you to your position," the boy in black says.

"My position?"

The boy shifts on his feet. "Yes, Miss."

I glance at Luca, and he nods as if I should go. "Maybe we could meet up later and visit the observation deck to get a better view of the planet."

"Um . . . I'm not sure—"

The blond boy taps on his tablet. "I can see Miss Foster's schedule is quite full tonight."

It is? What does he know that I don't? I strain to get a peek at his screen, but he drops the device to his side before I get a chance. Anyway, at this point, I don't care what's on the screen, since whatever is there is rescuing me from Hammond's assistant.

"Maybe another time, Mr. Powell," I say as the boy guides me away. But I really hope he never accepts the invitation.

"I'm sure we'll be seeing more of each other," he says. "And it's Luca."

"Mmm-hmm," I mumble.

The second boy leans into me once we're out of range. "You know . . . you should've just told him you didn't want to meet him on the observation deck."

I chew my lower lip. "It was that obvious?"

He chuckles lightly. "Oh, I'm certain Mr. Powell was oblivious to it. He's too busy trying to work his way up the food chain. But me? I have a talent for hearing between the lines." My savior turns to me slightly, and his lips quirk into a sweet smile. "I'm Max—Max Norton."

I grin. "It's nice to meet you. I'm Cassi—but I guess you already know."

"Yes," he answers, his smile shifting from sweet to amused. "It was on the schedule." He leads me to a row of ten empty chairs. Beside the seating gallery is the podium where Dad will make his speech during the unveiling. "Here we are."

"But no one is here yet," I say.

"They will be in five minutes or so, and you needed an out. I gave you one." He gestures to the first seat.

But I don't sit. Instead, I catch Max's upper arm. "Think you could stay with me until then? In case Mr. Powell comes back?"

He taps his tablet screen to bring up the time. "Sure, I don't have anything else to do." He raises his eyebrow.

He probably has a million things to do, but right now I don't care. I'm short on friends around here, and Max seems like a safe bet.

"So . . . how do you like your job on the . . . event management team?" I ask.

Max shrugs. "It's a temp job. A buddy pulled me in for the night. Most days, I help escort Board members and other bigwigs to meetings. Kind of like security, but not quite so important. I'm really more like a tour guide." He leans in. "You'd be surprised how loose people are with information around me, though. You'd think I was invisible."

Curiosity at his words creeps up on me, but I remain silent when a lady in a tall hat passes by where we stand. She takes her place in the row of chairs. It must be almost time to begin. I lean toward him and keep my voice down. "Like what?"

"Oh, mostly news of how the installation is going well on Arcadia. But, as I said, I'm good at hearing between their words. And then there's the tension." Max puts his finger to his ear as if he's listening to instructions in his comm.

"Tension?"

"Mmm–hmm," he mumbles, but I'm not sure if he's speaking to me or to the person in his comm. "Your father is coming out for the presentation in one minute. Would you mind taking your seat, Miss Foster?"

So, there are more influential people than just Dad who disagree with Hammond. Or, at least, have tension with her.

I nod but wish we had more time to talk.

"Thanks for helping me," I say.

"No problem. Enjoy the show." Max smiles, and I can only hope this isn't the last time I run into him. He gives me hope that maybe Arcadia won't be so bad.

"Ladies and gentlemen," a man announces over the sound system, and the room hushes. "Please take your seats. We are about to begin."

I turn and watch Max hurry away. The gathering of people mostly stops their conversations while they locate their assigned chairs around the dining tables. I lower myself into my seat in the special row, next to the older woman in the tall hat who had breezed past me just a minute ago.

She leans over to me as I sit. "The party is so exciting, dear."

Politely, I nod and fold my hands in my lap over the ripples in my puffy silk skirt. The rest of the "bigwigs"—as Max called them—file into the row, making me feel distinctly out of place. Hammond, dressed in a sequined blue gown, takes her seat at the opposite end from me. But when Dad steps onto the stage, looking handsome in his suit and still wearing the ruby tie tack, I let out a breath and relax.

The patrons erupt into thunderous applause.

Dad smiles and holds his right hand up to quiet the crowd. "I'll make my speech short because I'm fully aware it's not my face you're here to see this evening."

The gathering lets out a low chuckle at his joke.

"Thank you for joining me. I've anticipated this moment for the last decade, and there were days I thought our arrival might never come," he says. "But it has. While you were enjoying hors d'oeuvres and drinks, we very quietly dropped out of lightspeed and arrived at our new home."

Dad raises his hand high in the air. As if by magic, the floor-to-ceiling curtains fall and reveal a spectacular view of a blue and green planet flanked by two moons. A haunting mist of glowing cyan fogs over the globe.

Chills rush through my body. The crowd, including me, releases a collective gasp.

"Welcome to Arcadia," Dad says. "The salvation of the human race."

CHAPTER 3

"Why do I need to go down to the surface with you today? I can always go when the rest of the passengers do," I say to Dad as he leads me down the brightly lit white corridor toward the Skybase connector bay. "There's nothing for me to do except follow you around, cutting ribbons and stuff."

He gives me a look peppered with frustration. "Cassi, everything is a ceremony around here, and the passengers can't begin disembarking until the Board and higher-ups, such as myself *and you*, make the journey first."

I scoff. "It's not as if there aren't workers already down there. They've been building the city for two years already."

Dad tips his head and reaches into his jacket pocket, feeling for something but pulling nothing out. "You're just nervous."

Iciness from the corridor settles over me and I pull my sweater in a little tighter.

Seeing the planet last night was incredible, I'll admit that. But I want to tell him I'm just not ready to go down there without Mom. On the ship I at least feel like I don't actually have to face a new life that doesn't have her in it. I brush her gold band on my finger. This is all too final.

"But Mom—"

"Mom is why I'm so excited today." Dad's face softens, and he immediately stops walking and pulls me into an embrace. "There's something about Arcadia that brings me closer to her." His voice cracks with emotion. "When the curtain fell last night, I saw our dream right in front of me. It was as if your mother was standing right at my side, cheering me on and supporting me." He pulls back. "This planet is everything. *Everything*, Cassi. And I need you by my side to help everyone see there's so much more to Arcadia than we're even aware of. I know you don't understand yet. But you will. So we need to get down there. You're going to love it." His eyes sparkle in a way I haven't seen for over a year.

Confusion stirs in me. How could he know this for sure? This will be his first trip to the surface, too.

I nod and reach for his hand. "I'm with you, Daddy."

He smiles and gestures us forward.

When we arrive at the docking bay, a sizable group of anxious patrons wait to transfer onto the Skybase. After that, we'll board a transport ship and descend to Primaro, the lone city on Arcadia. I've seen all the photos and videos, and everything about the planet should be amazing. Each building is meant to mimic and blend into the existing nature to maintain the appearance that the planet is untainted by humans. Eventually, humans will expand over the surface, but Dad believes keeping everything contained is the smart thing to do until we learn more about how to successfully live on Arcadia. It was one of the few points of little contention between him and Hammond. But that was likely only because his plan kept costs down more than anything else. Hammond is a stickler for a budget. Not that anyone can fault her for *that*.

"Quite a crowd," Dad says.

From the number of multicolored jewels, gold, and expensive fabrics worn by the majority of the patrons, I know these people are the richest of the rich. They bought first dibs for the privilege of setting foot on the ground before any of the other passengers.

But then I see Hammond make her way to the front of the assembly and my excitement fizzles out. In contrast to the sequined dress she wore at the Gala, she's now dressed in a sharp black pantsuit and a pair of flat shoes. Her hair is pulled into a low, short ponytail. The hairstyle highlights the sharp angles of her face and pinched mouth. I glance at Dad, but he's admiring the buffet.

Lining the wall behind us is a massive spread of mostly untouched breakfast foods. Piles of bagels are loaded up on one end of the table, and bowls of cut and uncut fruit wait to be eaten alongside a variety of breakfast meats. The crowd's energy is nearly electric, and I can't help but let the excitement affect me. My mind buzzes with the activity.

I sneak another peek at Hammond and wind up staring straight into her ice-blue gaze. I quickly look away, shivering, but from the corner of my eye, I can see her motioning someone closer. Luca Powell appears, and she whispers into his ear. He pulls away with a quizzical expression and taps on his tablet for a brief second before rushing away without comment. Hammond's eyes locate the back of Dad's head and a sick feeling seeps through my stomach.

Before I have time to think much further on it, she steps onto a platform ahead of the entrance to the Skybase.

"Thank you all for coming today," Hammond says.

Applause fills the room, and Dad and I join in.

Hammond smiles coldly and continues. "We would not be here today without your generous support. As Dr. Foster stated last night," she looks to my father and nods, "Arcadia is our salvation, a chance to begin again and do it right. This new Eden will give the human race room to expand. We will thrive once again. And very soon, discover all the riches Arcadia has to give."

Arcadia does have much to offer. It's a lush planet, untainted by humans. The surface is loaded with new minerals, precious metals, and probably a number of undiscovered energy sources. But that bounty scares me, too. People are still fighting over how those things are best used on Earth, and the supply there is dwindling quickly. Money talks. Money makes the decisions. And how much people like Hammond are influenced by wealth, I don't know. As I study the patrons' dripping riches, I'm sure they want good returns on their sizable investments in developing Arcadia.

"Thank you again." Hammond's voice snaps me from my thoughts. "We'll be disembarking to Skybase in a few moments. Please be patient."

Hammond exits the platform. I link my arm into the crook of Dad's. At least there are still good men like him. He has a clear voice in this situation.

"I need to take care of something, Cassi," he says and wipes a bead of sweat from his forehead. "Wait here. I'll be back in a few minutes."

"Sure, Dad."

He pauses and removes his jacket. "Will you hold this? All the excitement is getting to me and I'm feeling a bit hot. You think you'll be okay?"

I take the jacket and nod for him to go. "No problem, I'll be just fine."

After he leaves, I spend a few moments scanning the bay, but the cavernous, white space is pretty boring without someone to talk to. And no one around here really wants to have a conversation with a teenage girl, even if she's Richard Foster's daughter. Maybe Max is here. He did say he performed a form of security for the "bigwigs," and these people are about as "bigwig" as they get.

I scan the crowd of maybe two hundred patrons and staff. But disappointingly, I don't see Max's spiky hair from here.

With a sigh, I check the space for Dad again. He had walked off toward the stage, but other than that, I'm not sure where he went. I know he told me to stay put. But there's no harm in poking around a bit for Max. Plus I want to grab a bagel since I forgot to eat breakfast this morning. Tired of holding his jacket, I thread my arms through the too-big coat and pull the fabric in close. I have no idea why Dad was hot. It's cold in here.

I stroll over to the buffet and pluck a cinnamon raisin bagel off the pile of assorted pastries. I scan the table for a topping like cream cheese, but I don't see any. No butter, no jam, no nothing. You'd think with such a lavish display the staff wouldn't have forgotten the spreads.

At the other end of the display stands a buffet attendant, his back to me. At least, I think he's an attendant. Most of the people here are probably used to being served, so it makes sense that staff would be helping. But his rumpled gray uniform isn't exactly what I expect from the quality the patrons demand.

"Excuse me," I say to him as I grab a plate and knife. As if he doesn't hear my question, he remains with his back to me. I try again, moving closer to his position, and speak over the room chatter. "Um, do you know if the buffet is out of cream cheese?"

This time, the boy with bronzed skin and jet-black hair swivels my way. Surprise washes over his face and he furrows his brows in confusion. He raises his hand to his chest as if to say, *are you speaking to me?*

"Yes, I need some help," I say. "I was searching for the cream cheese and wondered if you had any in the back."

His brown eyes grow wide, and instead of answering my question, he turns and dashes into the crowd of patrons.

I stand in confusion. What was that about? Maybe he's not supposed to be here. I drop the bagel, plate, and knife onto the table and follow him. To be honest I have no idea why I'm doing this, but curiosity overtakes me.

He's tall, over six feet, and I don't know if it's the unkempt uniform, but something about him makes him stand out from the crowd, even as he weaves through the people. Strangely, the scene is almost as if he's swimming through water, his moves are so graceful. And yet none of the patrons he avoids seem to notice him.

With ease he picks up his pace, but I do too, keeping my eye on him. The strange boy nears the edge of the crowd, and the opening to a corridor waits ahead of him. I'm going to lose him if he makes it there. Too many easy exit points after that and I'm not really familiar with this wing.

I speed up to catch him, and while moving full force, I accidentally slam into the shoulder of an older woman. She peers down at me in shock, and I'm pretty sure she's the same person I sat next to at the Gala last night. When her surprise wears off, she lets out a loud yelp from our collision. The boy whips around toward the sound. He looks at the lady and then straight into my eyes. And when we lock stares, a wave of freezing energy surges through my body. I gasp but quickly shake the sensation off.

"Sorry, ma'am," I pant.

The dark-haired boy tears from my gaze and spins away, rushing for the corridor. I push past the woman to get a visual of him again. I can't let him get away. Ignoring the complaining woman, I surge forward again. But when I reach the edge of the hall, he's gone— vanished.

Behind me and from the opposite end of the bay, a scream pierces my ears. Momentarily I forget about the boy and pivot toward the distress. I hope it's not that woman. I really only tapped her.

Before I have the chance to find out, a burst of orange and white light fills the room. A cry of help sticks in my throat as intense pressure, followed by heat, slams my body into the rear wall of the corridor.

CHAPTER 4

I blink my stinging eyes open to a wafting haze of gray smoke. Outside the corridor, a voice is shouting over the chaos, asking everyone to exit immediately through the south entrance. Then the emergency alarm drowns out all other sounds. I throw my hands over my ears.

What is happening? My mind spins as searing pain shoots up my neck and into the back of my head.

The smoke clears just enough for me to make out a few blurry shapes, if I squint. Beyond the corridor, people run around the bay while others lie still on the ground—hurt, maybe dead.

The memories rush back, and my chest tightens. A bomb! There was a bomb. I look down at myself to assess the damage and see Dad's jacket.

"Daddy!" I scream and wrench myself from the ground, despite the pain in my spine and head. When I stand, the room spins, but I force myself to stay vertical and drag my aching legs through the corridor's entrance.

The view is even worse than I expected. A large chunk of an internal wall beside the stage is blown wide open, and most of it lies on the floor. On people. Hazy smoke still fills the air, hiding the full extent of the horror. I cough and pull my shirt up over my mouth and nose.

A man runs past, and I snag his arm. He wheels toward me, his face full of panic.

"My father . . ." I say as my shirt collar drops down.

The man, whose clothes are gray with ash, stares at me with wide, blank eyes.

"Richard Foster—have you seen him?"

He shakes his head and pulls away from me.

"Help me!" I scream at the man as he disappears into the smoke.

Coughing, I sprint to the last place I saw Dad, when he was heading toward the stage. And now I can see it's exactly where the bomb exploded. The crack of a second eruption rips through the bay. I throw my hands up into the air in self-protection at the same time that a strong arm wraps around my torso, spinning me to the ground. The space around me transforms into a misty cyan, and a jolt of icy energy takes over my body. The room's chaos vanishes, and everything goes silent as if I'm in a protective bubble.

Am I dead?

An arm's pressure still holds me, and the cold turns to warm. My mind clears and my mission comes flooding back. Find my dad. I wriggle to loosen myself from the stranger's grip and shift to see who this person is.

It's the boy I chased through the bay. Being up so close, I get a good look at his eyes. Unlike the brown eyes I'd seen before, his irises nearly glow a deep cyan. His eyes are utterly magical.

"What are you doing?" I struggle against him, trying to forget the strangeness of his eyes. "I need to find my father."

The boy furrows his brows. I'd swear his eyes shift and become darker, almost normal. I'm imagining things. He opens his mouth to speak and then shuts it again. And instead of releasing me, he squeezes tighter. My head goes light.

I try to tell him to stop, but before I can do anything, the two of us are standing in the corridor I started in.

He spins me around and grasps my upper arms. "Listen, Cassiopeia, Richard Foster needs you to be safe."

Anger and frustration well inside of my chest. I struggle to free myself from him. "I know. That's why I'm trying to get to him. Let me go."

The boy's irises alter again with a slight cyan glow. Warmth overtakes my body and it's as if, this time, my energy connects with his. Our souls and minds dance together as everything else fades away. His eyes widen.

"He . . . he tried to make them understand," the boy mutters, and to be honest, I have no idea if the words are spoken out loud or straight into my mind.

He releases me, and with a snap of desperate loneliness, the connection severs, forcing me back to reality and into the horrible corridor. I inhale sharply as the boy disappears. Dizziness clouds my brain and I tumble to the ground in a heap.

"Cassiopeia!" Max shouts and drops to my side, appearing from the smoke. He gathers my torso up into his arms. "Can you walk?"

I want to tell him I can and that we need to go and find my dad. But none of the words come out. Only blackness seeps into my vision and the emptiness from the boy's vanishing consumes me. Then everything is gone.

Everything.

The strange-eyed boy comes to me in dreams colored in cyan. Tall and lean with powerful muscles and a haunting stare emanating sorrow. But when I stretch my hand out to him, he's always too far away, standing opposite of me across a vast chasm. Arcadia's two moons hang in the sky above, companions that are never without one another. Warm, humid air envelops my body, and I no longer need the sweaters I always wear.

I call to him, but it's as if he can't get to me either. I have so many questions in my mind. Why did he know my name? How did he know about my dad?

Oh, Dad. Where are you? Are you with me and now I can't wake up and get to you?

After what seems like years, I focus my mind and will my body to return to reality. I can't stay here. Finally, the blue-green world around me falters, and I watch as the boy blurs and fades across the chasm. The earth quakes under my feet, and I let out a scream. I rip my eyelids open to the white ceiling.

I gulp in a lungful of air and sit up. The room spins.

"Whoa, whoa, whoa," a familiar voice says, but it's not Dad's, and a hand reaches to my shoulder and guides me to lie down once more.

I blink several times and stare toward the speaker. As I do, my vision clears, and Max is next to me, tight-jawed. Sitting up on my elbows, barely, I realize we're in my room on the ship. My jewelry-making supplies are on the table next to me, and across the room is my computer and chair where I do my schooling. I glance down at my pajamas and then at my hand, which is tethered to an IV and attached to a bag of liquid hanging from a corner of my bed.

I dart my attention back to Max. "Why are you here? Where's my dad?"

The purple circles under Max's eyes tell me he might not have slept for a while. His lips form a tense closed-mouth smile, and he reaches for a pitcher on my side table. "Can I get you water? You must be thirsty."

I prop myself up again. The dizziness doesn't return, but my heart pounds while waiting for Max to answer my question.

"I'm not thirsty," I snap. It's a lie. The reality is my dry tongue is nearly sticking to the roof of my mouth.

Max pours water into a clear glass on my side table. His hand shakes, but he manages to fill the cup halfway and then sets down the pitcher.

"Can you sit now?" he asks. "Without a dizzy spell?"

I prop back up onto my elbows. "I think so."

He places his hand on my upper back and guides me up.

"Here, drink slowly," he says as he hands me the water.

I grab the glass and start to sip but then realize how thirsty I am and down the contents. I hold the empty glass out to Max. "More, please."

He flashes me a disapproving stare. "I told you to sip it."

"More, please," I demand. "And answer my question!"

Max snatches the glass from my hand and drops it to his lap. "I've been ordered not to tell you anything yet. It's not my place."

Fear churns in my stomach. And he was right. I shouldn't have drunk the water so fast. "He's dead?" My mind races with the possibility. Both of my parents can't be dead.

Max suddenly appears young, like a scared child.

"Tell me!" I scream and bolt up from the bed. I rip the IV off my hand and instantly regret it.

"I . . . I . . . I don't know," he stutters. "The Board won't release any information about the casualties yet."

"What do you mean?" I spin around and search for my clothes, but my mind can't put together what I should do next. "Can Hammond do that?"

"I don't know." Max stands and reaches for his tablet. "I need to call the doctor. I shouldn't have told you anything."

I seize the tablet and hold the device away from him.

A pained look crosses his face. "Cassi, I can't tell you anything else. After the explosion, transport shut down for two days—"

"Days? How long have I been asleep?"

"Four days," he says and holds his hand out to me, gesturing to the bed. "Will you please lie down?"

I hand him the tablet and partially obey his request by sitting on the edge of the bed.

"Transportation to the planet shut down for two days. But the Board isn't releasing any information about the bombing."

I throw my head into my hands, and Max lowers himself beside me.

"What about me? What am I going to do?" I cry.

Max shakes his head. "I don't know yet. There's only a skeleton crew left on the ship. Almost all of the passengers have transferred to Arcadia. If you didn't wake up after today, Hammond was going to transfer you, conscious or not."

"And why are you still here?"

He shrugs, and his eyes fill with compassion. "I guess I figured you needed a friend when you woke up."

Before thinking, I wrap my arms around his neck and sob into his shoulder.

I'm twenty thousand light-years from home, and all I have in the world now is a friend I barely know.

CHAPTER 5

I throw off my covers. My mind reels, forcing me to stay awake. I snatch the bottle of prescribed sleeping pills from my bedside table and throw it across the room. With a smack, the bottle hits the mirror behind my door. The lid flies open and the contents scatter onto the floor.

"Great," I mumble. But it's not like the medication was working anyway. Somehow, it's doing quite the opposite. The doctor has no idea why. Maybe I got too much sleep while I was out. But he does say I'm healing up nicely. There's barely any more pain in my back.

I glance at the time on my Connect.

3:36 AM

Apparently, Hammond is making me move tomorrow—well, today—and movers will arrive at 7:00

a.m. sharp to pack all my things. I can't stay on the ship any longer, she said. Part of me just wants to ask if I can take the ship back to Earth, but I know it's the wrong choice. Dad wanted me here. And I don't even know if returning to Earth is an option.

My throat constricts at the thought of Dad. Is he dead? Gone? Why won't Hammond release any information? I push the thoughts away, not emotionally willing to accept that Mom will never come home again, and now possibly Dad too.

Sighing, I get out of bed and grab for a pair of jeans from my drawer and slip them on. I drag off my nightshirt and pluck a navy-blue sweater off the floor and pull it on. Dad's jacket is draped over my desk chair and, without much thought, I tug it on to complete the ensemble.

I grab a hairband from my desk and use it to spiral my hair into a low, messy bun. I don't bother looking in the mirror. I already know it's bad, but there's barely anyone on the ship, and if they see the disheveled girl in the jacket two times her size, what do I care anyway?

I race through the unit as fast as I can. I don't want to see this place. Sitting on the counter in the kitchen is a plate of chocolate chip cookies Max brought me earlier. Logically, I know I should want to devour the entire plate since I haven't eaten in days. But the sight of the treats turns my stomach, and it takes everything within me to depress the gag rising in my throat.

I activate the exit and speed into the hall. My feet have a mind of their own and take me to Dad's office. I stand at the door and read the placard.

Richard Foster
Head Planet Terraforming and
Urban Development Engineer

I touch my index finger to the gold letters and my throat constricts. Then I move my hand down to the finger scanner on the door lock. Dad wasn't supposed to give me access, but occasionally he turned off his comm so I could find him if need be. He programmed my print to open the door, too. Maybe something inside can tell me what happened to him, where he is. I've ripped apart every drawer in the apartment and found nothing. And his computer is secured, denying me access.

The scanner beeps and flashes green. The door slides away. My heart sinks.

Other than a large desk and a chair, the room is empty. I hurry in and yank each of the four desk drawers open. Nothing. Not as if I really thought it would be any different. Why would the Board be so stupid as to take all of Dad's research but leave a few items in the drawers?

In one angry motion, I throw myself into the swivel chair and do a three-sixty, catching myself on the lip of the desk with a jerk. I pull my legs up into the chair and wrap the too-big jacket around them. Maybe I can just disappear, too.

I stuff my hands into the jacket's pockets, and a quiver rakes over my body as I touch an object inside of the right one. I touch the cool surface and pull out the item.

In my palm rests the most beautiful, deep cyan crystal that I've ever seen. Measuring about one inch long, the precise cuts on each side are incredible. I turn the gem over and inspect every surface. As I study the crystal, the room's coldness falls away and my body fills with warmth. The gem must be from Arcadia since I've never seen anything quite the same on Earth. Dad must've received the crystal from a building team that returned from the surface.

All I can guess is that he was going to give it to me since he knows I enjoy making jewelry. I clasp the crystal in my hand. So that's what I'll do with it when I get back to the unit. I know the perfect silver chain for it to hang on.

I stuff the gift into the front pocket of my jeans for safekeeping. As I do, I feel a presence come from behind. I gasp and swivel the chair to see who's there. But the office is still empty other than me, the desk, and the chair.

I shake my head. I'm just exhausted. And apparently delirious.

I rise and head for the exit but just as I reach my hand to activate the system, the door slides open and I'm met by a very sleepy-looking Max.

I let out a yelp.

"Whoa," he says and steps back, throwing his hands chest high in the air. His eyes open wide.

"You scared me," I say.

"Why are you even here at almost four in the morning? You're supposed to be resting."

I ease from the opening. "I can't sleep. I did tell you."

"Sleeping and resting are two separate things. And wandering around on the ship is neither." He crosses his arms across his chest.

I push past him and take a right. "You're not in charge of me, Max."

"No." He follows. "But I'm supposed to make sure you stay safe."

I stop and spin toward him. "And are you doing this out of the goodness of your heart?"

Max pauses and pinches his lips together.

"Did Hammond assign you?" With a huff I twist from him, but he grabs my arm, staying me.

"Would you rather Luca Powell? Because that's who she was going to assign until I convinced her otherwise." He stares me down with his gray eyes.

"What do you mean?"

"I mean what I said. She planned to have Luca monitor you. I told Hammond we had a good connection at the Gala and you trusted me."

I click my tongue. "Trust-*ed* you is right—"

"I've given you very little reason not to trust me. Okay," he says, raising his hands in self-defense, "I didn't tell you everything, but you've been a mess. It's not like you would've handled the news all that well."

I roll my eyes, but he's right. I'm not handling it well now.

"I haven't told Hammond anything. Not that there's much to tell. You really should go back to your room."

"I don't want to go to my room," I mumble.

Max expels an exasperated breath. "Then where *would* you like to go at four in the morning?"

I don't have any place in mind I want to go. "The arboretum," slips from my mouth.

"Okay. I haven't been there yet. Good of a place as any."

Without another word, Max escorts me to the arboretum's deck, and before I know it, I'm walking down the path beside the apple trees again.

"Wow." Max swivels his head, taking in the sights. "Too bad today's my last day on the ship. This is incredible."

The soft nature sounds calm me. And once again, I watch as the pigeon-sized bots zip from tree to tree doing their duty.

"Is it always daytime in here?" Max asks.

"As far as I know." I've never been here outside regular hours before. It's probably one reason the plants grow so well. I reach for a blushing apple and yank the fruit from its branch. Seeing it suddenly brings back my appetite, at least a little. "Want one?"

"Sure. Anything to get you to eat."

I grasp a second apple and pull, and it releases with a snap. I toss the apple to Max.

He catches it. "Thanks."

Something about the way he does it makes me smile for a moment. Max is sweet, and the fact is . . . I do appreciate him being here.

I bite into the apple and spot a bench about thirty feet from us. "Let's sit there for a while."

Max munches on his apple and nods.

"So, you must have been meeting with Hammond?" I say as we walk to the bench and sit.

"Her and a few other Board members. Not in person, but over a comm," he says, his mouth full of apple. "Hammond's on the surface."

"Has the Board released anything about my dad?"

Max gives me a patronizing smile.

I rub my face in frustration. "Okay, have you heard what caused the explosion?" Since I woke up, I've tried not to think about this, but voicing the words floods questions into my mind. The smoke, the sounds, the smell . . . the boy and his cyan eyes. A shudder works its way up my spine, but I shake the feeling off. "Was it a bomb? Was it an accident with the equipment?"

"Cassi, I'm seventeen. You truly think Hammond or anyone on the Board is purposely filling me in on top-secret details?"

I scoff. "There must be rumors, at least."

Max gestures around the arboretum. "And who would I hear these rumors from? I've spent most of the last six days with you, and there aren't many people left on the ship."

There's no way he's *only* commed with Hammond. The night of the Gala, he shared that he had a buddy on the ship. I do trust Max, but he's keeping information from me.

"Fine." I stand and toss my half-eaten apple onto the ground. An Agrowbot swoops in and gobbles the trash into its body cavity. "Then take me back to my room. I have to leave at seven, so I might as well get ready."

Max stands and flings his apple core and the same bot disposes of it. "Those things don't waste any time, do they?"

I raise my foot to walk but he places his hand on my shoulder, and I turn to him.

"Your dad would want you to face this challenge. He was . . . is a brilliant and brave man. And I'm pretty sure you take after him. That's the real reason I'm doing all this."

I tip my head in confusion.

Max crosses his arms over his chest. "I've always admired Dr. Foster and followed his studies over the years. When your mother was killed, I was devastated for your family. Everything seemed perfect, and then it fell apart."

My chest tightens. It was perfect.

"When I saw you at the Gala, I knew it was my chance to meet you." Max's face softens, and he looks down to the ground, his usual confidence diminished slightly.

"Why me and not Dad?"

He glances back at me. "There's just always been something about you, too. Anytime news stories would air and they showed your family. . . there was a strength about you. I liked it." Max touches my hand and quickly removes it. "I always thought we could be . . . friends."

My heart thuds in my chest and the ghost of his touch still lingers on my skin.

"I'd like that," I whisper.

"You want me to come in and help with anything?" Max asks at the door to my unit.

I wave my hand in the air. "I'm good. Thanks for asking."

He smiles. "Anytime. I'll be back in a couple of hours to escort you to Skybase. After that, we'll take a transport to the surface together."

The surface. The thought of it brings a lump into my throat, but I swallow it back. "See you then."

Max nods and heads toward the elevator.

"Oh, and Max?" I say, and he turns. "Thank you for getting me out of the bay."

He nods again. "You're just lucky you were in the corridor and not near the two explosions." He continues on his way.

I glance at my Dad's and my names still posted beside the door and quickly activate the pad to trudge inside. What now? There's no way I'm going back to bed.

I stuff my hands into the pockets of my jeans and locate the crystal I stowed there. I pull the gem out and stare at it again. My eyelids drift closed and a flashing image of the strange boy's face enters my mind. Not really his face; mostly his eyes that, for a moment in the bay, shared the same color as this crystal.

He's the one who led me from the first explosion and then rescued me from the second. There's no way I'd have come out uninjured, let alone alive. But my mind reels. I was right there when the second bomb went off. How did he get me into the corridor and at the right moment for Max to locate me?

I shake off my questions and open my eyes. I peer down at the multi-faceted crystal again and then jog to my bedroom.

On my night table lies the box of jewelry-making supplies. I flip the lid open and grab the tools I need. I also pull out the silver chain I've been saving for the right project. And it seems I've found just the one.

I flop onto the bed and spread out all the pieces and begin my work. This was Dad's last gift to me, and I won't waste it.

Today, I'll head down to Arcadia while wearing this pendant around my neck. And once I get there, the first thing I'm going to do is unearth what happened to Dad. Someone down there surely knows something. I won't give up until I find out who.

CHAPTER 6

'm stuffing the last of my clothes into a bag when a knock sounds on my cabin door. I check my Connect.

6:45 AM

He's early. With a flip, I shove aside the bag and walk through the unit to let him in.

"I'll be right there," I call out and tuck my new necklace inside my shirt. I'm not even sure I'm ready to share this discovery with Max.

I reach for the activation and hit the pad, and the door slides back. But the person isn't Max. I gaze up at a much taller boy who wears a casual white shirt, gray pants, and a smug grin—Luca Powell.

Instinctively, I retreat a few inches from the opening.

"Where's Max?"

Luca shrugs. "Reassigned, I guess."

I glance at my Connect again. There's no message from him. "Reassigned? He just told me a couple of hours ago that he was escorting me to the surface."

"I don't know anything about that, Cassi."

His use of my nickname tightens my chest. Only my friends and family call me Cassi, and I don't know him. Or even trust him for that matter.

"It's Cassiopeia."

"Cassiopeia." He smiles with mild amusement and my brows wrinkle. "Hammond sent me all the way from the surface to retrieve you. So, are you going to make me stand out here in the hall or can I come in?" Luca crosses his arms over his chest, smile still in place.

I ease away and gesture him into the living area.

Luca steps inside and scans the room. "This is a nice space. Twice the area of most cabin sizes."

I don't respond.

The smile slips away and he furrows his brows.

I don't think Luca is used to much resistance from girls.

"Look," he says softly "I'm trying to be friendly." I don't respond again, and after a few seconds, he sighs. "Are you ready to go?"

"I guess. I packed my bag and made a list of my Dad's and my things to be sent to the surface."

"Did you submit the order through your onboard account?"

I nod.

"Then the moving company should take care of all the packing." He waves me toward the corridor, a new confident smile in place.

"I need to grab my bag." I one-eighty, jog into my room, and pluck the bag off the floor. No way I'm leaving this behind. Packed inside is a framed photo of Mom and my jewelry kit.

"You know, the movers will get that too," Luca says when I near the entry door.

I thrust the bag into his arms. "Nah, you can carry it."

A shocked expression overtakes his face, and he blinks his eyes almost comically. "Now are you ready?"

"Yep . . . let's go." I march out the exit, likely never to return.

I stay several steps in front of Luca and type a message to Max.

What happened?

I hit send and slow down to let Luca catch up. Before he does, I check the message status, but it only states it's been delivered, not read. My heart sinks. I needed Max's support for this trip.

To hide my discouragement from Luca, I raise my chin and lift a single eyebrow as he removes my bag from one shoulder and flings it to the other. "Too heavy for you?"

"What do you have in this thing? Bricks?"

I scoff. "Yes—yes. I brought bricks from Earth."

Luca rolls his eyes and reaches my side. "Why don't you like me?"

I stop, and he does too.

"Mr. Powell. You must know my dad and Hammond don't . . . uh, didn't see eye to eye." The admission stabs at my stomach, but I continue. "Now, don't you think it's strange she wants you to play up to me?"

"I'm not—" His eyes widen.

"Of course you are. Whether you know it or not, that's what's happening." I cross my arms over my chest and tap my fingers in an irritated rhythm. "Now, why don't you tell me what happened to my father?" Heat creeps up my cheeks and I will the flush to stop since I'm fully aware my pale skin won't hide it. But it's no use.

"Cassi—Cassiopeia." He visibly swallows and looks away as if confused, but only for a single beat. Gaze now locked evenly onto mine, he says, "Even if I knew anything, I wouldn't be able to tell you unless Hammond okayed it."

"See, you *are* her servant." I flip around and storm toward the Skybase.

Once on Skybase, I let Luca take the lead since I have no idea where I'm going. We board a small transport ship owned by the Board. I grab my bag from Luca and cover my body with it. At least the covering makes me feel like there's more distance than the several feet between us. I turn and focus out the window as the transport glides toward the Skybase exit. The ship lifts off the ground, and in moments we're spaceborne.

The planet swirling with the cyan cloud of gas moves into view, and suddenly my chest grows warm. I press my fingers to the spot. My pendant.

I peer down and a faint glow emits from under my shirt. My breath hitches. I grab for my sweater's collar and fasten the top button. The green fabric is thick enough that the glow doesn't show through.

I whip my attention over to Luca but he's turned away, probably sulking.

I recheck my messages—still nothing from Max. I turn my attention to the planet again as it grows larger.

This is my new home, and I'd better get used to it. And with this thought, it's as if the cyan clouds permeate my mind.

"Miss Foster." A muffled voice resonates behind me and snaps me from a near trance. "Cassiopeia," the voice says again.

I turn my head and Luca stands over me. "It's time to disembark."

"Already?" I mumble, pulling on my bag, now pressed flat onto my lap.

"It was forty-five minutes."

I squint my eyes and take in the small space. When more clear-headed, I stand and follow him from the transport, still a little unsure of where the time went. I'm pretty sure I wasn't asleep.

Luca pilots me through the port and navigates us around several groups of people. At least he knows where we're going. My heart crashes against my chest, and strangely the air feels thick and difficult to inhale.

Luca turns to me as I lag behind and signals me forward. When I get there, he takes my bag. "The atmosphere is slightly different than Earth," he says, all business. "Everyone has a little trouble adjusting at first. But by the end of the day, you'll be fine."

We stride toward a broad wall of glass windows. Outside are ground transports and a scattering of people. But beyond the road is one of the most beautiful sights I've ever seen. The Tahm Range glistens in the sun, and below the mountain peaks is the skyline of Primaro.

Dad was right: the city does perfectly blend with the organic beauty of Arcadia. Plant life weaves through silver and white buildings designated for housing and office space. A few skyscrapers tower above the clusters of small- and medium-sized structures.

We exit through glass doors, and I'm met with a rush of warm air. My sweater quickly becomes too hot, but if my crystal is still glowing, I don't want anyone to notice—especially Luca. So, I leave the thick garment on.

Luca steps ahead to the curb and raises his hand. A few seconds later, a small vehicle pulls up.

"Our ride is here," Luca says as the door opens.

He leans in and places my bag in the middle of the seat and gestures me inside. When I'm settled, Luca slides in from the opposite side. He swipes at a small screen on the inside wall and then presses his hand to the computer. The screen glows green and beeps and then the vehicle drives forward.

"How long is the trip?" I mumble.

"Not long," he snaps, probably annoyed by my lack of desire to be around him. Luca taps on his Connect and a hologram pops up. He keeps his attention on the display as he texts words I can't see. Probably reporting to Hammond about my sour disposition.

I turn my attention to outside the window as we depart from the port. Up close, the city is even more stunning. Not too far up ahead, I glimpse how the builders wrapped plant life across the buildings in intricate patterns, perfectly melding the organic with inorganic. The city is small enough that many people can walk to their destinations or take public transportation. The streets are busy with pedestrians and a few self-driving vehicles, like the one we're riding in now. A sleek commuter train zips off in the distance. Even a white sanitation bot hovers over the sidewalk and scans for trash and debris.

Our transport takes us deeper into the city until, after about a fifteen-minute journey, the vehicle stops in front of a tall building. Not a skyscraper, but at least twenty stories high.

My door slides away, and I grab my bag.

"Is this it?" I ask Luca over the top of the vehicle.

Luca nods and motions me to the entrance. "I need to be at a meeting soon. So this will be quick."

"Fine by me." I clutch my bag and follow him as I gaze up at the building and sky. Instead of the blue on Earth, the sky on Arcadia has a cyan tint. I'm pretty sure Dad told me once, but I probably wasn't paying much attention.

I follow Luca inside, where he has already used the call button for the elevator. The doors slide open, and we take the cab to floor seven.

I know Dad showed me photos of our on-planet unit, but I wasn't paying much attention then either, since I didn't want to go. Now I wish I had.

We exit the elevator and end at a door marked "740."

"Well, here you go," Luca says, hesitating to meet my eyes. "Place your thumb on the lock pad. That's your key."

I do, and above the pad a small light shines green as the lock beeps. The door clicks and I enter my new home.

"Hammond or I will be in contact, if need be." Then he turns and walks toward the elevator.

I swing my attention to him. "Wait. That's it? I have no idea what I'm doing here." Ugh, maybe I should have been nicer to him.

Luca spins on his heels but keeps walking backward. "Your roommate will fill you in on everything."

"Roommate?" I turn and face the opening again, and inside is a studio apartment. I sweep my gaze around and take in a set of bunk beds and a small kitchenette. "Dad and I had a full apartment provided!"

Luca shrugs and turns away again. "The situation has changed. That apartment has been re-allocated." He disappears inside the elevator while I'm still in the hall, now alone.

I pinch the bridge of my nose and close my eyes. Re-allocated? Meaning: Dad's gone and I'm no longer valuable. After a beat, I open my lids and gasp when I see a young girl with dark skin and hair standing in the doorway. Although her face is young and fresh, something about her eyes appears much older.

"You shouldn't just stand out there," she says.

"Where'd you come from?"

"A girl goes to the bathroom, comes out, and has a roommate now." She gestures me inside.

I exhale slowly through clenched teeth and then follow her suggestion. Once inside, I scan the small space again. A few dirty dishes are stacked precariously in the kitchenette's sink, and my forehead wrinkles.

"Don't mind those," she says. "I wasn't expecting anyone."

My lips thin into a frown and my stomach sinks. Hammond has apparently taken everything from me and there's not anything I can do about it.

"Let me give you the tour," she says and points to the bunk. "Bedroom. You get the top."

Great. I would've loved that when I was ten. Absently, I twist Mom's ring and gnaw the inside of my lip.

Quickly she directs me around the open room. "Kitchen, office, living room, bathroom—and we're back at the bedroom again."

The "office" consists of two thin chairs and a fold-down desk with two laptop computers called DataPorts, while the "living room" has two small, padded chairs and a media screen affixed to the wall. Next is another door, which must be the bathroom. The whole space can't be more than two hundred square feet.

"I'm Irene, Irene Parks." The girl holds out her hand to me.

I reposition my bag on my shoulder and reach out to her. Irene clasps my hand and shakes it with more vigor than I'd expect.

"And you are?" she says and releases me.

"Oh . . . I'm Cassio—Cassi." I decide not to give her my last name. From her demeanor, I'm not sure she knows yet, and since I'm not familiar with her, I don't want her feeling sorry for me.

Irene eyes my bag. "You can put that down, Cassi."

"Oh, yeah." I dump the bag next to the bunks.

"You got other stuff coming?"

I nod. "But I'm not sure how I'm going to fit everything in here."

"Then you'll need to pay to store it."

"Pay?" Dad always took care of the finances. I have no clue what I'm doing here.

Irene sighs. "You know . . . like CosmicCoin."

"Of course. Where do I access my account?" Whether or not Hammond has transferred my dad's funds is another issue, though.

She gestures with her head toward the DataPort. "That should be connected to your ID and thumbprint.

You can log on and check." She raises a brow. "This was all discussed in orientation . . . were you asleep?'

"Just overwhelmed."

"Well, I get that. What's your job assignment?"

I stare at her, speechless. Assignment? Sure, I've been training in planet terraforming, but it takes years to learn everything. And Arcadia already has Dad's development plan.

She clicks her tongue. "You better get it together fast. We're all expected to pull our weight around here. I work in the tech lab at Extra Solar. If you don't figure out a solution, Hammond will have you confined."

The hair at the base of my neck stands on end. As Richard Foster's daughter, I was never one of the passengers who risked being jailed for failing to secure a job. But now I'm no one. Anger mixed with terror churns in my gut. How did any of this happen? How could my life be such a mess, and no one really cares? I press down the thoughts because if I don't, I might explode.

"I'm just tired," I explain with a faint shrug. "I haven't slept in a few days."

"Well, your luxury suite awaits." She indicates the top bunk. "And I have errands to do anyway."

Irene grabs a messenger bag off a hook by the door. "See you later, Cassi."

I exhale deep and long with exhaustion and then climb the ladder to the top bunk, where I quickly bury myself under the comforter. I twist toward the wall and pull out my pendant and rub the surface between my fingers. It's no longer glowing and just looks like a regular crystal, albeit an unusual color.

How am I supposed to uncover anything about Dad if I'm not sure what's even going on around here? As I hold the crystal, a sensation of warmth and safety permeates me. Maybe this is what Dad meant when he said the planet made him feel closer to Mom. My eyelids droop, and I drift into dreams of a blue-green world.

CHAPTER 7

I log onto my computer and check my account. Apparently, Dad had prepared for the possibility of something like this happening. Without me knowing, he had set up a year's worth of CosmicCoin in an account under my name. The sum is a modest amount, enough to cover my basic expenses. I'll need a job in the next couple weeks, though, simply to pay for any extra needs.

I stare at the number and sigh. Even with Dad gone, he did the best he could to make sure I'd be okay. And the funds mean that I won't have to worry for a while about being sent back to Earth against my will.

I log on to check the status of my belongings. I use a small amount of my funds to have Dad's and my long-term stuff put into storage for now, at least until I can figure out what to do with it. But the tracking number is nonexistent. I send a help message to find out what's going on.

On top of that, my personal items haven't arrived at the dorm yet, either. I tap the link to see what's taking so long.

Arrival delayed. Expected delivery time unknown.

"Well, that's encouraging," I mutter. At least I brought most of my clothes in my bag, and Irene let me borrow a few toiletries.

"As long as you pay me back," she had said.

Before I forget, I transfer currency into her account. Don't want my roommate mad at me the second day I'm here.

I log off and close the DataPort's lid. I've been so used to fancy computers with glass touchscreens that this basic model feels positively ancient. But I guess the Board wouldn't stay in budget if they provided top-notch equipment to the planet's workforce. And it will do for now. I should be grateful the computer was here in the first place.

I rise and study the cramped room, pinching my lips together. Irene is at her job already, so I can't have her show me around the city. Well, standing around here does nothing for me either. I might as well use the time while unemployed to see if any rumors are circling about the explosion or Dad's disappearance. People should be talking about the incident, I would think.

I grab a pear from a bowl of fruit on the kitchenette counter and head out the door.

For the last time, I check for any messages from Max. Still nothing. What happened to him? I want to be mad, but part of me knows whatever went down was not his fault. He would have been here for me if he could. Hammond has to be involved.

What's her problem? My dad was the one who made it possible for her to even bring people to this planet. I have no clue why she'd be treating me so poorly, no matter what their differences.

I push the thoughts away since they'll only distract me from my goals.

Out on the street, I inhale a deep breath. Amazingly, the air feels good. Clean. Luca was right that I'd adjust to the atmosphere quickly. Most of the air on Earth has grown bad from pollution, especially in the cities. I was lucky Mom and Dad made sure we kept our home in the country where the air remained decent. But even with that, I'm not sure I knew what I was missing.

The air on Arcadia fills me with life as if it's strengthening me. I throw back my shoulders and lift my chin. Now, if I only knew where to start.

As I scan my new surroundings, pedestrians hurry past me, probably to work. A silver airship cuts across the sky to transport either people or supplies to another part of Primaro. A few blocks over I spot the tallest building, and I can only assume it's the Board's headquarters. Many of the other metal and white clad structures are labeled with corporate names. Some I'm familiar with, others I'm not.

Irene *did* mention that Extra Solar was only a thirty-minute walk from the dorm and she didn't want to waste her currency on paying for the train. That's why she left so early this morning.

The street is busy with pedestrians and as I scan their faces, a person across the street catches my eye. He stands a few inches taller than the rest of the people, and unlike the pedestrians, he's standing still, as if he were a river rock allowing rushing water to flow past him. His hair is nearly black, and he stares my way with dark eyes. The same boy from the bay. The one who ran away.

My heart thuds so loudly that I'm positive anyone on the street can hear it. The skin under my crystal grows warm. *Don't be glowing. Don't be glowing.* I want to look, but if I take my attention from him, he could bolt.

"You have information," I whisper to myself and start off in his direction.

He remains still for a beat; but as I check the street for vehicles and step off the curb, he does precisely as I predicted. I pick up the pace and don't let him out of my sight.

No chance you're getting away this time.

Newfound energy races through my veins as if I were a track star. As if running for sport was what I was born to do.

My feet pound across the street to the other sidewalk as I watch the boy take a passage between two buildings. My mind abruptly flashes with new information. Without a second thought, I tear into the building in front of me, nearly tripping over a sanitation bot. There's an exit out the back, and I can head him off. I have no idea how I know, but I'm not going to question it.

I weave through the people inside with ease and follow the map in my mind toward the rear of the building. I slam my hand to the lock and push the door open. Using a final burst of energy, I surge outside, and the boy skids to a stop right in front of me.

His eyes widen, and before he has the chance to escape, I grab his arm.

"Stop running," I growl, panting for breath.

The boy looks at the spot at my neck where the pendant hides under my shirt. Not letting him go, I glance down at the glowing gem and then back at him.

His shoulders rise and fall as he regains his breath, too. But he doesn't fight or attempt to escape. It's almost as if his feet are frozen in place. He's tall with a broad chest and shoulders, and I'm instantly overcome by his strength despite his inaction. I know he could break free if he wanted to.

As I clutch him, my hand grows warm, just like the crystal's sensation. My chest tightens with emotion. Sadness, fear—terror. But the feelings are not mine.

I choke back tears and grip him tighter. I'm not sure, though, if keeping a hold is for comfort or to keep him from escaping.

"You—you know what happened on the ship," I force myself to say while pushing away the unwanted emotions.

But he doesn't answer.

I lock onto his eyes as the dark irises seem to swirl with cyan.

"Tell me!" I shout. "You know what happened to my father!"

The boy's brows wrinkle with concern, and for some reason I'm certain it's for me, for my dad. "Your father was a good man." His voice is deep and rich and curiously filled with song. At least, that's the best way for me to describe his speech. The melody behind his words seeps into my very being.

The space around us warps, causing me to close my eyes to center myself. But when I do, my mind transports to another place. Memories that aren't mine flood my brain. A woman with a soft smile and cyan eyes comforting me in her tender arms. I sink into them until just as fast as the first came, another memory replaces it. I run with my friends through the forest, laughing without a care in the world. Joy, sadness, pain, loss, wonder. Thousands of feelings and experiences latch on and become part of me.

Clicking steps echo behind me and rip my attention from him, and without thinking, I release the boy's arm. The rush of memories halts, but their imprint remains. A blond girl in a blue dress, close to my age, approaches from ten feet away. I turn from her and stretch for the boy again, but he's halfway down the walkway, and with him, the intense energy I had experienced in his presence. There's no way I can chase him down again.

The girl speeds up and stops by my side. "Are you all right?"

I point toward the boy who's still in sight. "He got away."

She looks the way I'm pointing and turns to me, eyebrow arched. "Who got away?"

"The boy who was just here," I say, raising my voice. I glance back toward the walkway to find he's disappeared.

"Um . . ." The girl, who stands several inches shorter than me, gnaws the inside of her lip and blinks her eyes nervously before saying, "No one was with you. I could see you from all the way back there." She gestures to the way she came. Then she brings her hand to my forehead.

"At orientation, the speaker said that in rare cases we might feel a little sick for a few days. Maybe you should go home and lie down."

I slap her hand away, still reeling from whatever just happened with that boy. "I don't want to lie down."

"Whoa, fine. I'm just trying to help. I saw you arrive at the dorm yesterday and figured you were still trying to figure things out," the girl says, her hazel eyes staring me down.

I relax my shoulders. "I'm sorry. You must be right." I don't want this girl to think I'm crazy, even though there's a good chance something isn't right with my head. "I haven't slept well in the last few days, and I have no idea where I'm going in Primaro."

She smiles. "Believe me. We're all still learning. How about if I show you around? I had an interview today." She glances down at her dress. "And I planned to explore the city myself. Oh, I'm Alina, by the way. Alina Morse."

"I'm Cassi."

"Well, we better get going, Cassi. In a few, there's a gathering I wanted to see in the square a couple of blocks from here."

"A gathering?"

Alina nods. "President Hammond is making an announcement."

Hammond? Not as if I want to see her, but maybe I could speak to her about the investigation.

"Yeah. That's a good idea," I say. "Thank you."

"No problem." She continues walking the way she was originally heading before she stopped for me.

I know the boy is real. There's no way he's not. But how did he know my dad? Or that he was a good man? My heart skips with hope.

Alina leads me down a street a few blocks over. She talks the entire way, but I barely hear a word. I'm too busy hunting for the boy, but he's nowhere in sight. Overhead is a faint outline of the two moons hanging above Arcadia. They still haven't disappeared into the morning light. One is larger than the other. It's going to take time getting used to this alien view.

As we approach the square, more and more people gather, but Alina wants a front row view and pushes her way through the crowd. I just follow, figuring the closer I can get, the better chance I have of earning Hammond's attention. After several dirty looks, we arrive at the front of a portable stage and in direct line with a metal podium.

Cheers come from the crowd behind us, and I turn around to see why. To the left, on the street, a large white vehicle slows. The door has the Board's emblem on the surface. It must be Hammond.

The transport rolls to a stop. Two large men dressed in black exit from the front and flank the emblemed door just as it slides away. Luca steps from inside, followed by

Hammond. Her lips turn up into a tight smile and she motions to the crowd, which immediately bursts into applause. Luca and her guards fall in behind her as she proceeds toward the stage. Once behind the podium, she raises her hands to quiet the enthusiastic crowd. Many still clap and roar with an occasional cheer.

"I am so privileged to join you today." Hammond gestures to the two moons. "Can you believe what an amazing place our new home is?"

Of course, the crowd erupts again, and she has to do the thing with her hands to quiet the people down. While she does, I flip my attention to Luca, who's staring my way. But when our gazes touch, he looks to Hammond and clasps his hands loosely in front of his waist, shoulders straight back. The two guards in black take up space below the stage at each corner and wear expressions apparently meaning business.

Beside me, Alina is just as engrossed in Hammond as the rest of the crowd.

"You all are the heart of Arcadia. Your dedication to transform our new planet into a home that humans can be proud of *is* the very foundation this relocation project is built upon," Hammond says. Hanging her head a moment, she waits a fully charged second before facing the crowd once more and saying, "We all share a great sadness over the explosion on the starship *Pathfinder* and those who died."

My stomach tightens. Maybe she *is* going to give us some information.

"Please know that we are doing everything we can to examine the explosion's cause," she says. "But so far, investigation shows this just to be a terrible accident."

I pump my fist at my side. She must be lying.

Hammond goes on for at least fifteen more minutes, but I don't hear much of it. All I want is a chance to give her a piece of my mind. But she's probably going to return to her vehicle as soon as the speech is done, a feeling I can't shake.

I lean into Alina. "You said you live in the dorm, right?"

"Yeah . . . 725. Why?"

"I don't think I can do our tour today."

"Sure, okay." She returns her attention to Hammond.

"Excuse me," I push past the people in the front row and head toward the vehicle. All I need to do is be in her walkway, and then I can get her attention.

"Thank you, thank you," Hammond says, and I pick up the pace to make sure I have a clear view of her for when she comes down the stairs.

I keep my attention glued to her location and press past a few more people. "President Hammond," I shout.

She turns to me and locks eyes. Immediately, one of her guards steps in front of her.

Hammond sighs, and reading her lips from across the stage, I can see she tells him, "It's fine," and then she waves me forward.

I step toward her. "Tell me more about the explosion in the bay."

"Miss Foster. As I've already shared, the Board is working on it, but so far the details are classified. You know I can't give you what you want, let alone in this setting."

I knit my brows. "Richard Foster's my father, and I deserve to know what happened to him. You stuck me in that dorm with no information. It was cruel!"

She hushes me and gives a tense smile to the people around us. From behind her, Luca steps from the crowd and leans in to her ear.

"We need to go, President Hammond," he says.

"Yes." She turns her attention back to me. "When the investigation is complete, you'll have any information I'm able to release. But I make no guarantees."

"But—"

"No, Miss Foster. The explosion was unfortunate. But it happened. Be grateful you have a roof over your head and food in your mouth. Now go and make a new life here."

One of her guards eases toward me and touches the weapon on his hip.

Hammond turns to Luca, her nostrils flaring. "Would you please escort Miss Foster to ensure she makes it safely from the gathering?"

Luca motions to me, but I quickly spin on my heels and storm through the crowd, my palms sweating.

Was that a threat? Why wouldn't I be safe?

CHAPTER 8

Through the swinging door's small window, I check that no one is coming and then push open the white swinging door from the kitchen. In my hands are a tray of plated chicken and roasted potatoes and a medium rare steak with a side of green beans. The food's smell wafts up into my nose and makes my stomach growl.

Three days ago, and right after I spoke to Hammond, I received a message that I was assigned as a server at Spectra, the only fine dining restaurant so far in the city. I suppose it could be worse.

Still . . .

Only one more hour until my shift is over.

In a few seconds, I arrive tableside to the well-dressed couple with my best fake smile. I learned quickly that if you forget to smile, patrons tend not to tip you much at the end of their dinner. In graceful motions, I place the ordered food in front of the diners.

"Enjoy your meal." I lay on the thick, sweet tone. "Is there anything else you need?"

The man looks at the woman and then shakes his head. "No, I believe we are fine."

I nod and turn toward the kitchen to retrieve an order for my second table, when a person catches my eye. A dark blond boy dressed in a sharp suit enters the restaurant.

Max! My heart skips with excitement. But it quickly stills since I still want to be mad at him.

He glances around the room and spots me. His face lights up, and any anger inside of me melts. Max is just far too nice to justify any lingering offense.

"I'm sorry," he mouths before my supervisor, Suzanna, approaches him. Then he turns his attention to her and starts a conversation I can't hear.

Taking as few steps as I can toward the kitchen, I watch out of the corner of my eye as Max shakes Suzanna's hand and points to me. She glances my way and nods, then gestures Max through the restaurant.

Soon enough, Max is by my side. "Go into the kitchen. I'm supervising as you pack a to-go order for the bigwigs."

The two of us push through the doors.

"Where were you?" I say as the doors shut behind us. "And why didn't you answer my messages?"

Max tips his head. "You think I did any of that on purpose?"

I sigh. "No, I was just checking."

"Ever since Hammond shuffled me off the ship, I've been looking for you. All my contacts were deleted off my Connect. I finally got a tip-off last night when one of my assignments mentioned a friendly girl with long strawberry blond hair as their server."

Well, at least my act makes an impression on a few people.

"I was a little unsure about the friendly part, but—" Max smiles and I smack him in the arm. "But other than that, I was pretty sure it was you."

I shake my head at him. It's good to have Max back. "But what are you doing here?"

"I convinced today's assignment that having a fancy meal sent to their quarters for a working dinner meeting would be a good idea. Earlier in the day, I had overheard him saying how he wanted to try the food here."

Remembering my other table, I glance up at the screen on the wall, displaying the completed meals. It's not ready.

"What's your order number?" I ask.

Max taps on his Connect. "Thirty-six."

I recheck the screen. "Okay, it's still going to take about ten minutes. But I can start the salad." I lead him to the salad station and pull on a pair of disposable gloves.

From the side, one of the other servers gives Max a strange look. Probably because he shouldn't be in the back.

"He has to oversee the order for a client. Suzanna cleared it," I say to her.

She shrugs. The restaurant patrons tend to be picky, so she apparently accepts my explanation, grabs a basket of rolls, and then returns to the restaurant floor.

"Suzanna did clear it, right?" I lean into him.

Max nods. "But we don't have a lot of time, and I have information for you."

My stomach drops as I grab the recyclable container for the salads.

"Did you find out something about the explosion?" I whisper and peek over my shoulder to ensure none of the other staff are nearby. "Or about my dad?"

"Not yet," he says. "But the last of the Board are arriving from Skybase today. Hammond decided to keep a few of the members onboard until all of their offices and housing had a thorough sweep with additional surveillance installed."

"And what does that mean for me?"

Max tips his head. "Not all of the Board sides with Hammond all the time. There are one or two you might be able to plead your case to. Lia Hirata and Lawrence Cooper would listen to you."

I load the containers with lettuce and other salad ingredients. I glance at the order screen again for the dressing types and pour the correct ones into their dishes and snap on the lids.

"I tried talking to Hammond the other day," I say. "She has guards all around her, and then I ended up here." I gesture around the kitchen. "I've never served food, and the first day I nearly got myself fired. I'm pretty sure Hammond is happy for any excuse to send me back to Earth so I stopped asking questions. What do you think would happen if I try to approach a Board member in broad daylight?"

"Well, I would never suggest you talk to them in broad daylight," Max says. "I have pretty good information that those two work late into the night at their offices. And might be meeting without Hammond tonight."

A small amount of hope swells in my chest as I load the salad containers into a delivery bag. "And you know the location?"

Max's lips curl into a devious smile. "And I have the codes to get you into the Capitol building."

"Are you coming too?"

He shakes his head. "No, you're going to need to do this on your own. I have an assignment, and you need to move quickly before you lose your chance."

I glance to the screen again and see that both of my tables' orders as well as Max's to-go order are ready.

He taps his Connect and holds the device to mine. "There. I sent you the codes with Hirata and Cooper's office locations. The building codes change daily, so tonight is your only chance for this. I don't know if I'll be able to get access again."

I throw my arms around his neck as tears sting the corners of my eyes. "Thank you," I whisper into his ear.

"It's the best I could do. I'll make sure to be in contact soon."

Suzanna steps into the kitchen. I immediately release Max and step around him to retrieve the ready orders.

She raises her eyebrow but says nothing, and then moves off in the opposite direction.

All too soon Max is gone with the delivery bag in hand, and I'm back on the floor apologizing for the lateness of my table's meal. But the couple is quick to forgive when I give a sweet smile and promise a slice of cheesecake when they finish.

After my shift ends, I message Irene that I won't be home until late. I have no idea if she cares, but I figure informing her is the polite thing to do.

The two moons hang overhead, making the sky considerably brighter than on Earth. Stabbing pain shoots from my toes and into my feet from hours of standing, but it's only about a fifteen-minute walk to the Capitol building from the restaurant, so I do my best to ignore the sensation.

A few pedestrians mill around on the street and the train is still running. But overall, the city is much quieter than the morning bustle. Most of the jobs are long hours, and my guess is that a lot of people are simply tired. I know I am. If Max hadn't shown up today, I'd probably have gone straight to bed when I got home. If that's what the dorm is—a home.

As I walk, I twist mom's ring on my right ring finger while I mull over the plan I made for once I get into the building.

I'm still wearing my serving clothes and have my work ID for Spectra. The instructions Max gave will lead me through the service entrance in the rear. The guards change shift right at 8:00 p.m. I should be able to slip in then. If I get caught, I'll just tell them I was hired to serve at a meeting held tonight. The plan is probably a terrible idea, but right now, it's all I can come up with.

The map on my Connect leads me down to what appears to be a shortcut through the backside of a few buildings. Native plants twine up building surfaces in random patterns and recolor the wall's metal gray to various shades of green. I run my hands along the leaves to calm my nerves and notice how the vines boast tiny white flowers now twisted closed for the night.

As I graze a bud with my fingertip, a faint glow comes from beneath my chin and I look down. The crystal is glowing again! Another light catches my eye and I halt all movement. The flower beside me has opened and emits a soft cyan light. I turn and see that all of the flowers on the metal surfaces behind me are now open and glowing.

Well—this is a terrible way to try and sneak into a building.

I pull my hand away from the leaves, but it's too late. Whatever action I put into motion is already well on its way. On the building in front of me, the flowers dotting the structure's metal walls are lighting up, one by one.

A lump forms in my throat, and I do my best to swallow it. But no use.

The building I need is two blocks over. Maybe if I don't touch anything else, I'll be fine. I stuff my hands into the pockets of my pants and pick up my pace. All the while I try to ignore the glowing flowers that seem to be traveling up the building and onto the next layer of foliage. Maybe it was a coincidence. I don't know everything about the plant life on this planet and maybe what happened is totally normal.

I reach the building's end and step out onto the street when a tall, thin man with pure white hair nearly walks into me. I jump back and throw my hands shoulder high into the air. The thin man turns. But it's as if he stares straight through me before pivoting away. Odd. His hair is white as if he's very old, but his face seems younger than Dad's.

I knit my brows in confusion. "Sorry about that. I guess I was distracted."

The man whips his head around and mutters a few words in a strange language, one I've never heard before. The words lilt in a way similar to the strange boy's voice. Like music.

Almost out of nowhere, a young woman appears on the street before me. She's older than me, but not by much. Her long wavy hair is dark, but I can't tell the exact shade. Under the waning light, it's difficult to discern much about her. But I can see that her skin appears rich, like a tan, and her features eerily remind me of the strange boy.

The girl uses her hands when she speaks, and I can't understand a single word. But by her rushed tone and the tension in her jaw, I can tell she's anxious. And by the calm tone of the man's response, it seems as if he's attempting to reassure her reasons for distress.

I shouldn't stay. But their language reminds me of the boy. The ship did carry a significant portion of international passengers, most of whom do speak English as a second language. They could know him.

"Excuse me," I say, fully aware this is a terrible time to get their attention. But it might be my only chance. Who knows if I'll see these people again.

But the two only continue their conversation.

One last try. A little louder.

"I'm wondering if you could help me locate a person. I think he speaks your language."

Still nothing.

I throw my hands into the air when, beneath my chin, the crystal glows again. I start to raise my hand to hide it, but immediately the girl and the man spin my way and stare directly at me. My heart instantly kicks into a gallop and thuds against my rib cage.

The man speaks with his melodic accent. I have no clue what he says, but for some reason all I want to do now is leave. I try to lift my foot, but it's stuck to the sidewalk.

In a blink, the man vanishes and then reappears directly in front of me. I gasp as his face grows pinched and he rattles off a few phrases, his tone now terse.

"I don't understand you," I yelp and throw my hand to his chest.

Just as my palm makes contact, the girl lunges for me and her hands wrap around my throat. My brain tells me to scream, but I can't.

I thrust my hands out to make her stop, and as I do, a shadow enters from the corner of my vision. A figure rips the girl off me, and the two bodies crash to the ground with a thud.

I grab my neck while struggling to breathe.

The white-haired man backs away from the two fighters. My savior jumps to his feet and pulls the girl with him. I get a good look at his face—the boy.

He pushes her and yells words in their language. Breathing hard, he swivels his attention between the two people and points to the left and down the street.

The girl glances at me and narrows her eyes. My breath hitches when the irises swirl with cyan for a split second. But the two turn and race down the street, and then disappear into the darkness.

The boy turns to me, his chest still heaving. "I'm sorry about them."

CHAPTER 9

"Sorry about *them*?" I rub my neck where the girl's fingers had wrapped around it a moment ago. I try to clear my throat, but it aches as I swallow. A shiver shudders down my spine with the memory of her hostile expression and swirling irises.

"What about *you*? I've only been trying to talk with you about what happened on the ship, and all you do is run away."

Across the street, two people walk together, casually glancing over here. The boy whips his neck toward the couple and back at me.

He lowers his voice and gestures us into the walkway behind the building. "Well, I'm not running now."

"No way!" I dismiss him by waving my hand. "I'm staying out here where everyone can see me." Part of me wants to trust him because of the connection I've shared with him, but the other part thinks the whole thing could be an illusion.

The boy, dressed in a loose light-colored shirt, maybe tan, lets out a sigh and shakes his head. "You wouldn't say that if you knew what was going on."

I step toward him and he eases away, keeping his distance.

"That's exactly what I want to uncover—what's going on," I growl.

The boy throws a nervous glance in the people's direction, but the couple is now out of sight.

"Who *are* you?" I demand. "And who were that man and girl who tried to choke me? I've had enough threats lately. I don't need any more."

"Someone else threatened you? Who?" he asks.

I don't answer. No way I'm going to tell him about Hammond at the gathering.

The boy's eyebrows knit together, and with genuine concern in his expression, he reaches for my neck. But he lowers his hand and instead says, "Are you okay?"

"No. I'm not okay." In fact, I can still feel the girl's hands squeezing me as if I were still a threat to her. "And you should hang around different people! Who are they?"

The boy stares at me and says nothing for far too long. "I can't say," he finally says. "But I can help you in another way."

Frustrated with him, I cross my arms over my chest. "You ran away from me the other day, and now you want to help?" Part of me wants to push past him and say forget it. But my options are so limited. If he has any information about my dad, I should let him say it.

"If you can't tell me who they are, how about you start by telling me about you?" I ask.

He shakes his head.

I scoff. "I can't trust you if I don't even know who you are."

Conflict brews in his eyes as he whispers, "My name is Javen."

My chest fills with electricity upon hearing his name. I clutch my shirt, right over my heart, with the sensation's suddenness. Visions of Javen from when I was unconscious whirl through my mind like a movie in fast-forward. His name is like music to me, a "haven," just like his name suggests, and everything in me wants to trust him. To be with him—*what am I thinking?* I barely know this guy. I blink and push all the feelings and memories away. But the best I can do is let the sensations simmer just under the surface.

"My name is Cassi," I choke out, unsure of how else to respond. Then I remember that he already knows my name. Memories rush back of when he protected me in the corridor.

He bores his stare into me and I know, despite all logic saying otherwise, that he's having the same set of intense, heart-pounding feelings as me.

"I know your name . . . Cassi." The way my name forms on his lips nearly draws the air from my lungs. He blinks and adds, "I can get you into the Capitol building."

I step back, hit by the reality train. How does he know where I'm going? Max and I are the only people who made these plans. Maybe this is a trap. My pulse quickens, now for different reasons as my mind reels between the decision to forget the whole thing or get away from this boy and go on my own.

"You're never going to make it in without my help," he says as if he had read my mind. "The codes the male gave you will work to get you in. But Hammond installed too much security. You'll be caught within five minutes."

My pulse picks up even more and now pounds in my ears. "Male? You mean Max? What else do you know about me?"

He peers at the ground. "Enough."

"Are you following me or Max?"

"Not exactly."

"Well, then *what exactly*? Suddenly now you want to help me?"

"Cassi," Javen says, "I'm sorry about the other day. But the time wasn't right. I didn't know enough yet."

His words are so confusing. "Time for what?"

"I wish I could tell you and I do apologize for that, but as you noticed my . . . friends are not too happy about you." Javen points the way the girl and man went and then lowers his hand to his side. "Right now, I can help you get inside the Capitol building and out safely. That's it. But I do know you will be unable to speak to the Board members you were searching for."

"Why not?" He even knows who I'm planning to meet?

"Because on the way here, I saw them leave the building."

My heart sinks. What good is it to get into the building if I can't ask Hirata and Cooper for help? "Then forget it." This is too weird and breaking in isn't going to work anyway.

Javen thinks for a few seconds. "I could get you into Hammond's office."

I open my mouth to protest, but it's not a terrible idea. In reality, it *is* a terrible idea, but I can't let my quest for truth die since that is exactly what Hammond wants. And there's something about this boy that makes me want to trust him.

Most of my logic cast aside, I gesture forward. "Lead the way."

Javen guides us around the back of the Capitol building. The plants wrapped around this building do not appear to have any flowers—leaves and vines only—which is a relief. Despite the moons, the overhead light is dim. Thankfully there are no other people in sight. I scan the wall for any surveillance and find no obvious units. Doesn't mean there aren't any, though.

As we use the walkway, Javen picks up his pace and raises his right hand. "There, the building's security cameras will begin to loop. But we don't have much time. Altering the feed for too long will appear suspicious."

So, there *are* cameras. I have no idea what he just did, but I doubt he wants to get caught either, so whatever. I'm going to trust he adjusted the surveillance.

We come to the service entrance per Max's instructions, and I start to tell Javen the code. But before I get there, he hovers his hand over the lock and the door pops open.

"How'd you—"

Javen is already piloting me inside the building before I get the words out. The space we step into is plain, as I might expect a service entrance to appear. He looks around and holds out his hand as if to tell me to be quiet.

I guess that's something to ask about later when we're not in a hurry. But he must be using crazy spy tech to hack the building.

"It's safe," he whispers. "We have several minutes before the guard arrives."

I shake my head, having no idea if he's right or just lying. And if he *is* lying the joke really is on me.

To the side is a staircase, and Javen motions to it. I check a map outlining Board member office locations in the information Max sent to my Connect. Luckily, Hammond's office is only five floors up in suite 516 and not in the penthouse. Maybe she's afraid of heights.

Javen and I race up the stairs, and once at the exit to floor five, he stops me again. His head turns from side to side several times as if he's listening.

"It's clear," he says.

"So, you're telling me that you can hear whether or not the coast is clear?" I ask, catching my breath.

His dark brows push together. "Of course."

Of course! As if everyone has super hearing. I shouldn't trust this guy at all because this is crazy. But for some reason I do. I shrug and push open the door into the white-walled office corridor. Overhead, a few dim lights illuminate the space. I scan the hall and then turn right to locate suite 516. I see the office next to a door marked "Briefing Room."

I race to the correct door and allow Javen to release the lock. It's faster that way. After he does his thing, the door slides back and we both hustle inside. My heart pounds with the hope I may find information about Dad. But the hope is quickly dashed when I take in the room. The whole space is pretty sparse: a desk, one office chair, and two extra seats. No artwork decorates the white walls, or anything else for that matter. Light from both the city and the moons stream in through the large window, making it fairly easy to see. On the desktop is Hammond's touchscreen computer. That's my best bet.

"Can you get into her computer?" I ask since I know nothing about hacking and he seems to be an expert.

Javen looks toward the computer. "Possibly. But I'd need more time than we have."

Okay. Change of plans. I sprint to the desk drawers and throw them open, one at a time. But mostly they're empty. A few office supplies, personal items. Nothing that would give us any information about the explosion or my dad.

"She must have all the information all locked up in there"—I nod to the computer—"or she takes anything useful with her when she leaves."

I plop down in her seat and motion to activate the power. Javen quickly blocks my action with his hand.

"Her log in might have an ID scanner. It could pick up on your fingerprints, DNA . . . anything," he says. "Let me see what I can do."

Javen leans in and powers up the tech. The glass lights up, and a new Board symbol splashes across the screen: Earth and Arcadia overlapping while surrounded by stars. Despite having no clue why he can log in and not me, I stand and allow Javen to sit. Instead of using the projected keyboard, he runs his hand in front of the screen and from his fingers comes a slight glow. He closes his eyes and the logo disappears. Computer code moves across the screen faster than I've ever seen. Javen's eyelids pop open, and he watches the scrolling as if he can decipher the information that quickly. No one can, though. It's not humanly possible. I throw my hands into the air. This is useless.

"Let's just go," I say, before my attention moves to the bottom of the screen to a blinking icon. A blinking icon that wasn't there previously. As I watch, a glow comes from below my chin. My pendant blinks at the same rapid pace.

Why is it doing that? I rest my fingers on the crystal and try to figure out what's going on. Then reality hits me. An alarm is going off. We triggered a security alarm.

"Javen." My voice comes out in a shaky whisper, but he doesn't answer. It's almost as if he's in a trance. "Javen," I repeat, this time louder.

He blinks down hard and the scrolling code stops.

"We tripped an alarm!"

Javen spins toward me in his chair. "That's impossible." But then he moves his attention to the crystal pulsing under my shirt collar and his eyes grow wide.

"We need to get out of here. Now," I say.

Javen springs from his seat and holds his hands out to quiet me. He tips his head as if to listen, again. "I should've never logged on," he mutters. "I knew there wasn't time."

There's no place to hide in here except for under the desk, so I run to the door. But before I get far, Javen grabs my upper arm and I whirl toward him.

"We have to go now!" I yell as I pull for the door.

"Cassiopeia." Javen's voice is calm. Way calmer than it should be in this situation. "The guards will be here in twenty seconds and they have weapons. We can't make it. But I can get us out of here."

Twenty seconds? I scan the room again. There's not even a closet.

Javen steps forward, keeping his fingers wrapped around my arm, and gently pulls me close to his chest. My head spins with his scent. It's like the fragrance of a clear day right after the rain.

"We can't do this." I fight the urge to melt into the safety of his body. "If the guards catch us here,

Hammond will detain me, and I'll never find out anything about my dad."

But Javen only pulls me in tighter, and his hands rake into my hair. I look up, and he inhales deeply. He leans down and presses his face against the top of my head and whispers into my hair, "Trust me."

Trust him? What is he going to do? Make us invisible? I try to pull away but can't. Javen's strong arms hold my body in place until he hurries us up to the window. Still clutching my upper arm in one hand, he throws his free hand forward and emits a cyan-colored blast, blowing the window out from the inside in a deafening roar. As if the scene were in slow motion, the glass shatters and rains onto the deserted street below.

I let out a yelp from the sound. Javen snakes his hand around my waist in one fluid motion and forces me up onto the now-open ledge. Wind blows my hair away from my face.

I glance down and my stomach churns. We're only five floors up, but I'm unconvinced we're going to live if we jump. Might as well be the thirtieth floor, for all it matters. Javen glances behind us and grips onto me tighter.

"Hold your breath and jump, Cassiopeia," he says as a blue-green glow radiates from us.

I want to say there's no way I'm going to do this, but just as I open my mouth to speak, the door to

Hammond's office flies open and hits the wall in a resounding crack. Several laser blasters target the window and the blue beams shoot past me.

Javen leaps from the ledge, pulling me into the air.

I don't even scream.

CHAPTER 10

This is it. My life is over.

The words circle in my mind.

I squeeze my eyelids shut and brace for the hard pavement and certain excruciating pain, but instead my body is plunged deep into water.

I gasp and the shock sends liquid down my throat. I throw out my arms to swim as my eyes shoot open. But of course, I can't see anything in the pitch-black pool. My lungs burn like fire. Air, I *need* air.

But I have no idea which way is up. I could be diving deeper for all I know.

My lungs burn for oxygen. Trying to right myself, I kick my legs behind me. But as I do, a pair of strong arms grabs for me and we start to ascend. At least I hope we start to ascend.

Javen and I burst out and onto the surface. I choke, gasping for breath and coughing up water.

Looking around, everything is gone. The city, the buildings, the street, any people shooting at us. Overhead are Arcadia's moons, but the sky sparkles with cyan wisps that were previously not there. Surrounding the river is a thick forest packed with lush vegetation. Beyond the trees is the same mountain range near Primaro. Everything appears so strange. As if the landscape is a cooler color temperature than I'm used to seeing. But I'm not sure if that's it.

"Whe . . . where are we?" I sputter as he drops me onto the shore.

When searching for Dad in the ship's bay and then, suddenly, before the second explosion, Javen was there. And then I found myself in the corridor with him. Can he teleport? I'd thought maybe I'd imagined that, but there's no way this is all in my mind right now. I glance down at my soaked body and server's uniform and push a clump of dripping wet hair off my face.

Beneath the collar of my shirt, the crystal glows brighter than ever and illuminates the night-sky darkened earth below me.

I wrench my arms up and turn toward Javen, who's sitting next to me, his chest heaving.

"What happened?" I demand once I've caught my breath. "Where are we?"

Javen drops his head into his hands and says nothing.

"Javen," I say. "You blew out an entire window with a blue-green glow that came from your hand. People were shooting at us. You threw us out of a window over a street and we ended up in a river. That's not normal. You need to tell me what's going on."

"I'm sorry it had to be that way," he whispers. "Normally I would have cloaked us . . . but it doesn't protect against the lasers . . ." His voice tapers off, and then he groans and slumps to the side and onto the ground in a heap.

My chest tingles with fear. "Are you okay?" I scurry across the grass and sand on the shore. His right shirtsleeve is torn and bloody, and beneath the tear is a significant wound. One of the blasts must have hit him. I pull the tear open further to examine the damage. With a grunt, I roll him over onto his back and search for any more possible injuries. But there's nothing else.

I turn him around and recheck the wound on his arm. The cut isn't bleeding anymore and all I can think of is that the laser fire must have cauterized the laceration. But what's left *is* angry, raw and red and, by his clenched jaw, causing him intense pain.

"How far are we from the city? I can go get you help."
But he lies still.

Could the wound be worse than I think? My mind races. I can't let this boy who saved me die here, in the middle of nowhere. I nibble my bottom lip. You can't die from an arm wound. Can you? But something is still wrong.

I stand on shaking legs. My head spins as if I'm not receiving enough oxygen, much like when I first arrived on Arcadia. But in a few seconds, my mind clears and I study the area. Other than the mountains, nothing is familiar. And there's no way I can make it through a thick, dark forest on my own.

My Connect—I can message for help! I look at my wrist and tap the screen. Nothing. It's blank.

I grit my teeth in frustration and shake the device, then recheck it. But the screen is still black and won't activate. The device is either damaged from the water or we're out too far from the city for the device to work.

Javen stirs and taps my leg with his hand. I bend down next to him.

"What can I do to help you?" I ask as my eyes sting with sudden tears. "Do you have a way to message someone?"

His eyes lock onto me and his irises fade from their dark brown state to swirling cyan. My eyes widen as I draw in a sharp breath. Everything about his face is the most beautiful I've ever seen, from his angular features, the way moonlight touches his coppery skin, to his full lips. His eyes . . . oh my, those eyes. If things weren't so messed up, all I'd want to do is fall into his embrace, allow the night to wrap around us, and kiss him. The memories that must be his flicker in my mind and I feel as if I know him—I've always known him.

How can this be when we've only just met? The whole thing is crazy, and I know it. I push the feelings away. There's no way they are real.

He reaches up and brushes my cheek with a trembling finger, taking away a fallen tear. Just the caress centers me, and the fear in my core dissipates.

But then he winces, and his grimace shoots me back to reality. Javen gestures to the still-pulsating crystal around my neck.

"I need your Starfire," he whispers.

I pull away from him, not understanding his gesture or his request. "Starfire? What are you talking about?"

"Your—necklace. Can I borrow it?"

I push my brows together in confusion.

"The energy inside will heal my wound . . . and restore me from the shift, but I need to apply the crystal directly . . . to my arm." His voice becomes so low that I barely hear him. I lean in closer. "After that jump I need to . . . renew. I'd use mine but"—he hisses in pain—"we don't usually carry one across because the healing only works on this side."

He must be delusional from the pain, but I'm not sure what other options I have. Despite my reservations, I reach in and pull out the pendant from my shirt. After I unlatch the clasp, I place the necklace in his hand. The second I release the pulsating crystal, the world around me carousels. Javen is still in front of me, but he's fading in and out. My lungs struggle for air as if I'm drowning again. I fall forward and catch myself on his chest. Immediately, the spinning stops, and I watch as he places the crystal to his arm while I roll off his chest to the side of his injury. The area surrounding his hand glows for a few seconds, then goes out.

Javen inhales deeply while straightening his spine. The strength in his body returns and he holds the necklace out to me. I dip close to his face and allow him to clasp the pendant around my neck.

"Thank you," he whispers.

Amazed, I glance at the hole in his shirt. The skin underneath is completely healed. "How does that work?"

Javen shushes me. He swivels around as if he heard a noise. Then he jumps into a low squat. I listen for whatever the sound is he thinks he hears. But other than water lapping onto the shore, it's completely silent out here.

"You have to go," he finally says and stands.

"Go?" I look around. "Where? I don't even know which direction the city is in."

Concern fills his eyes, his irises now a normal color. "They'll be here soon."

I shake my head in confusion. "*Who's* going to be here soon? Maybe they can help. How do you know they're unfriendly?"

Javen holds his hand out to me and pulls me to my feet. "Because I know. My . . . my friends can't be aware of your presence."

My mind flashes with the memory of the glowing-eyed girl who tried to choke me. Maybe he's right. If all his friends are like that, I don't want to meet more.

"Fine," I say as I attempt to wipe the grass and dirt from the sides of my pants, but the stains are too bad. And I'm still too soaked.

Javen pulls me toward the water and my pulse picks up.

"Are we going back that way?"

"No," he says. "It won't work again. But you need to follow the river."

I pan over the wide, slow-moving river and then swing my gaze back to him. "What do you mean 'me?' You're not coming? I'm going to get completely lost."

Javen grips my hand tighter and laces my fingers with his. "I promise. Your Starfire will lead you through the Intersection if you follow the river. It shouldn't be long, and you'll find the path to return to your home."

I narrow my eyes at him. Intersection? Nothing he says makes any sense. We're nowhere near the city. "*Please* come with me."

"I must go the other way to ensure they don't detect you." With his other hand, he reaches up and grazes my cheek. "I can't let them." The touch makes me want to melt into him. Still holding my hand, he squeezes it. "They shouldn't, but if anyone tries to approach you or speak to you, keep moving as if you don't see them."

"Javen, you have to tell me what's going on here. If people want to hurt me, how will ignoring them help? And I'm ninety-nine percent sure the river won't lead me to the city."

He tenses his jaw and opens his mouth to speak, but then he whips his head the other way. "You must go now. Don't let anything stop you."

Defiant, I cross my arms over my chest and don't move.

"Cassiopeia, if you stay, I may not be able to protect you. I promise that I'll explain all of this to you soon. I'll track you again by summoning your Starfire." And with that, he spins me in the direction he wants me to go and gives me a gentle push. "Now go."

I twist my head around to ask when soon is, but he's gone. How did he do that? Well, what choice do I have now? My heart races as I take off along the shore, following the river.

CHAPTER 11

The farther I go, the stranger this place becomes. My pendant—what did Javen call it? Starfire? Well, whatever the crystal is, it hasn't stopped glowing since I left him . . . or *he* left me. And I'd swear the water beside me keeps shimmering with lights. But every time I turn, the glow is gone, like an apparition in my mind. Luckily, I haven't seen a soul. Although there have been a few strange bird calls I've never heard before. I don't even want to think about the animal life on Arcadia. A few nocturnal wolf-like creatures exist that could gobble me up in minutes.

Up ahead, the trees seem to thicken, and I'm having second thoughts about continuing. Where would I go anyway? Javen said the journey shouldn't take long and I've been walking for around fifteen minutes.

I pick up the pace again and jog through the trees beside the water. As I walk, my crystal grows even brighter, and beside me, the flowers on the trees open and close, illuminating the night as they do. Just like the flowers on the buildings in Primaro. My breath shakes and everything around me fades in and out. The same experience as when I gave Javen the pendant. My stomach churns with the sensation, and I take a deep breath, realizing the air is becoming thin again. Logic tells me to turn back; this place isn't safe. But Javen's words float to the surface of my mind.

Your Starfire will *lead you if you follow the river. Don't let anything stop you.*

I propel myself forward and through the thick trees. The farther I go, the denser the foliage becomes, the leaves, branches, and vines scraping against my body. But I push forward, believing I'm going to get to where I need to be, even though the hairs standing on end at the back of my neck tell me otherwise. Until this moment, I had never felt so alone, so unprotected. If one of those wolf-like creatures attacked, would anyone in Primaro miss me? What if Dad isn't dead and can't find *me*? I draw in a shuddering breath and blink back the forming tears. I miss Mom. She would know what to say to me right now. She would know how to comfort my fears. I lift my eyes to the stars and, for a moment, pretend that she can speak to me, tell me where to go and how to find Dad. A heavy sigh leaves my body and my shoulders droop. I twist the gold band on my finger and gnaw the inside of my lip. Then I lift my eyes back to the trail along the river, determined to push forward, and freeze.

A faint glow comes from up ahead, and I focus on it. The strange light wasn't there before. I look back up to the stars, wrinkling my brows before focusing on the light, moving my feet forward with renewed confidence. I reach for the illumination and push away a branch. Instantly, the world returns to normal, and I'm standing on the sidewalk directly in front of my dorm building. My chest clenches, partially with relief but mixed with utter confusion. I make a one-eighty and the forest is gone. There's nothing but the buildings across the street.

Maybe I'm the one who's delusional! My Connect vibrates, and I look down to a message from Max. It's working again.

Are you okay? Message me back. I should never have let you go alone.

I have to get off the street first. Who knows if the authorities are out searching for the people who broke into Hammond's office. And if the authorities already identified me, I guess I'll find out when I get to my room.

I sprint into the building and take the elevator to floor seven. Once I'm there, I scan the hall for any activity, but the space is silent. I walk to my room, my feet still squishing in my shoes. At the door, I thumb the keypad and the door clicks open.

The inside of the room is dark except for a small crack down the curtain's middle, which streams moonlight into the center of the space. Irene must be asleep. I tiptoe in, not wanting to wake her.

"Where were you?" Irene's voice comes from the darkness.

I jump and let out a tiny yelp. "You scared me."

She snaps on the light under her bunk and stares out at me, pinching her lips and furrowing her brows. "No one had any idea where you were, and—what's his name again?—Oh, Max . . . Max stopped by. He's cute by the way, nice too, and you don't come across many guys like that. So, of course when he was at the door, Alina noticed from her dorm room and came over."

I stand, not knowing what to say to her. Anything that comes out is going to sound completely crazy.

"I . . . I just wanted to see the city."

"Max told me who you are. You're Richard Foster's daughter."

I sigh and look away from her. "Yes."

"He died in the explosion."

I swing my attention back to Irene. "We don't know that. No information has been released." It's stupid to say, though. Of course he's dead.

She nods, and the expression on her face reflects momentary guilt until she returns to being all business again and continues. "Alina said that you approached Hammond at the gathering the other day. And from what she could tell, your confrontation didn't go well."

"No, it didn't," I mutter.

Irene throws off the covers and swings her legs to the ground. "I hacked into the city security system. An alert was released on how Hammond's office was broken into earlier tonight." She walks over to me and wrinkles her nose. "Why are you wet?"

My stomach tightens and then flips. I run a hand through my still-damp hair and eye my rumpled, dirty, soggy clothes. "I . . . I, uh, don't really know how to explain any of tonight."

Irene shrugs. "Well, at least there's a measure of honesty in that. Not something I'm used to." She nods to the bathroom. "Why don't you take a shower? Then we can talk more when you get out."

I nod, realizing I can't wait to get out of my clothes. I grab pajamas from the drawers next to the bunk and head for the bathroom. With the door shut, I start the water and peel off my uniform, tossing the clothes on the floor.

I step into the shower and sigh when hot water flows over my body, washing tonight's events away. My mind drifts to Javen. I picture his face and wavy dark hair in my mind. The way he speaks to me is a sound that mixes words and music and I have no idea how or why. The way I feel when he touches me . . . my entire being longs to be back with him. He said he'd contact me soon and explain everything. Why can't it be now?

I shake my mind from thoughts of him.

How can any of this be real? Did I really break into Hammond's office? Breaking and entering? That's not who I am. And then love at first sight with a guy who's—no, focus Cassi. You just met him! It's just a weird infatuation.

I reach for Mom's ring on my finger and study the shiny gold. She'd be so upset with me right now for my behavior. How could I let her down? I grab the shampoo and rub a dollop into my hair to distract myself from my anxiety while working the suds into my scalp. But Mom's disappointed face is all I can see in my mind.

Yet how can I let her down by not finding Dad? That's more important, right?

I don't have an answer. If solving this gets me killed, Mom wouldn't be very happy about that, either. I sigh and bend my head back beneath the spray of warm water as Dad's words before the Gala rush back to me.

If I teach you one thing—always follow your principles. There are times when no one will understand your reasoning.

"I need to hold my ground," I mutter. There's no way I'm letting the explosion and whatever happened to Dad get swept under the rug. After tonight, I know that digging up information could get me killed, but I need to find out what happened and what Hammond knows.

I finish showering, dry off, and then slide into my pj's. Before I open the door, I close my eyes and tuck the pendant under my shirt. *Dad, if you can hear me. Please help me get through this.*

My lids slowly open and I stare at the door handle. What am I going to tell Irene?

I twist the knob and swing open the door, and steam wafts into the living room in a big puff. Irene is sitting on one of the so-called chairs with her legs draped over the side. She spins toward me.

"You look better." She eyes me up and down. "Now spill it. You can't live in this room with me unless I know what's going on."

I gulp down my nervousness. I could move out and not tell her a thing. But moving isn't what I want. Right now, I need stability. Maybe if she's aware of what's going on, she can help. I take a seat in the chair next to her and begin.

"It wasn't well known, but my Dad didn't get along with Hammond at all," I say. "The two of them had completely different viewpoints about making Arcadia a home for us."

I tell her the entire story of how I eavesdropped on the secret meeting when Hammond surprised Dad. Irene listens without interrupting the entire time, just nodding and totally engrossed.

"So, you think the Board might have caused the explosion to try and kill your father because of his opposing views?" she finally asks when I'm done.

I nod. "I can't prove anything, but if the explosion was just an accident, why isn't Hammond releasing any information to the public?"

"I'm not even going to ask why you were all wet when you came in, but did you break into Hammond's office tonight?" she asks.

"No," I say a little too quickly.

Irene stares at me and I just know she's going to declare that I'm a liar and make me leave, or perhaps that I'm in shock or that the Board is trying to do the right thing—

"None of this surprises me."

My heart skips with hope. "What? Really?"

"At Extra Solar, I get access to the higher-up projects. Nothing top secret or anything, but the projects made me curious. And curiosity made me dig. When no one was watching, I hacked into the company system and learned . . . let's just say *eye-opening* information. I've always had to watch my back, and I can't let my guard down here either."

I lean closer to her. "What have you found ou—"

A knock echoes at the door, and I swing my attention to our dorm's entry. What if Hammond found out? And now she's here. "Who's that?" I ask.

"How am I supposed to know who's at the door in the middle of the night?" Irene scoffs as she rises. Without even using the peephole, she swings the door open—Alina.

The blond girl looks as if she just rolled out of bed, and considering the time, she probably did.

Alina yawns. "Did Cassi come home?"

"You came over here in the middle of the night just to ask if Cassi came home?" Irene asks.

Alina shrugs. "I woke up and couldn't go back to sleep. So, did she?" She peers around Irene and spots me. I wave. Instantly her eyes open wide, and she pushes her way past Irene.

"Excuse me?" Irene says, raising an offended brow, but Alina doesn't pay her any attention and plops herself down into Irene's vacated seat.

Irene closes the door and pulls up one of the computer desk chairs, all the while glaring at Alina, who still doesn't notice Irene's body language cues.

"So, where were you? Were you meeting with a guy or something?" Alina says, suddenly completely awake.

"A guy? No," I choke out. But why would she say that?

"Well, then *what*?" Alina asks.

Maybe I could tell her, too. Really, she's been nothing but helpful. She tried to take me on a city tour, and she's checking in on me now.

I open my mouth to speak.

"Did that guy Max happen to message you?" Irene interrupts.

I swing my attention to Irene, and she shakes her head slightly.

"Max is really cute," Alina says with a sigh. "You think he's single?"

Maybe more than one confidant is a bad idea for now. I follow Irene's lead. "As far as I know, Max doesn't have a girlfriend."

Talking about boys seems to make Alina forget all about her original question.

"Are you into him?" she asks.

The question takes me aback. I haven't even thought about Max that way. He has been nothing but sweet and helpful. And she's right; he *is* good looking. But I'm not here for boys. Especially after everything that has happened. A relationship would complicate everything further. Not what I need.

So why can't I get *Javen* out of my mind? My insides quiver with just the thought of his name. "No," I say, almost too forcefully. Softening my voice I add, "Max and I are just friends." I'm not sure if that statement is entirely true or even how Max feels, but figuring that out is way beyond my emotional capacity right now. Stifling a yawn, I mutter, "You know what, though? It's late, and I'm super tired."

"I have to be at work early, too," Irene says and looks a little grateful for the change in topic.

Alina checks the time. "You're right. Glad you're okay, Cassi."

"Thanks for checking in. Good night," I say and head for my bunk. I scale the ladder and, once I'm up there, throw the blanket over my head.

The door opens and shuts. I peek out to see if Alina is still here—gone. I let out a relieved breath.

"We still have talking to do, Cassi Foster," Irene says.

She's right. We do. But I say nothing. Instead, I place my hand over the Starfire and wait for sleep to come.

My Connect buzzes and my eyelids flutter open. I bring my wrist to my face and squint. It's Max. My stomach does a flip when I see it.

Where are you?

I completely forgot to message him.

I'm so sorry. I'm fine. Can we meet later?

I send the message and another returns almost immediately.

I can be there at 11:00 AM.

I check the time; already it's nine-thirty.

See you then.

I swing my head down to the bottom bunk. Irene's bed is already made, and she's nowhere to be seen. I'm not sure how she sneaks out of here so quietly or gets up so early in the morning without waking me up. But I scurry down the ladder and change from my pajamas into a white T-shirt and a floral skirt. I caress the green sweater in my drawer but decide against it since I haven't been cold since I left the ship. Without much thought for the style, I run a comb through my hair, brush my teeth, and then I'm out the door.

In the lobby, I head straight for the exit, but through the window I spot Luca. He's getting out of a black vehicle with the Board's symbol etched onto the door. Maybe Hammond knows I was in her office.

I one-eighty and speed walk toward the elevator. I palm the call button and glance above at the screen displaying the elevator's location. Ugh. It's still several floors up. Instead of waiting, I turn to take the stairs. Maybe I can hide on the stairwell until he's gone.

"Miss Foster," Luca's voice calls out from behind.

I stop in my tracks and slowly spin toward him. What am I going to say?

Think, think.

He stops a few feet in front of me. "I'm so glad I caught you. Do you have a few minutes? I need you to come with me."

A shudder runs down my back. I could run, but what good would it do?

"Um . . . okay. I was leaving to do an errand."

"This won't take long."

I glance around the foyer and outside. His vehicle is gone, so it's not as if Hammond is arresting me. Relieved but wary, I reluctantly nod and follow him. I have a feeling that declining isn't really an option, despite his attempt at politeness.

Luca and I walk for about three blocks before he says anything else. "So, how are you settling in?"

Now that's a stupid question. "How do you think I'm settling in, Luca?

"I was just trying to be polite. You know, small talk."

"If you want to be polite, put in a good word to Hammond about me. It isn't kind to keep information about my father from me. And I've done nothing to deserve unkindness. *Nothing.*"

Luca stops in front of a building and considers me a moment. "Well, you're also holding back from us."

My jaw clenches at his words and I look past him to where he's led me—the Capitol building. *They know.* A knot forms in my throat. I wasn't paying attention along the way at all.

"Holding back?" I ask, trying to keep my voice steady.

A faint smile plays across his lips. "Why didn't you tell Hammond you'd been training as a terraformer under your father's supervision?"

My body relaxes and Luca tilts his head, waiting for me to reply. A lock of wavy brown hair falls over his unnerving blue eyes, which continue to watch me closely. When my thoughts catch up with me, I say, "My studies weren't official or anything, so I didn't think it was worth mentioning. Especially since it takes years to become an expert."

"Well, Hammond viewed your training sessions through your father's account, and she thinks you're good enough to start a new project." The faint smile grows.

My mind shouts *no, no, no,* and I gaze up at the building in panic, when a thought hits me. "The job, it's here?"

He nods.

"I'm still not certain of my skill level, but I'm willing to try."

Luca fully smiles now. "Well, that was easier than I thought. I'm glad you're seeing things our way. You'll begin the day after tomorrow."

If you only knew, Luca . . .

"I'll take care of informing the restaurant of your new employment. What do you think about meeting for dinner there tomorrow night to discuss the details?"

Without a thought, I take a step back. Apparently, my body wants nothing to do with that request either. But Luca is a means for information.

"Sure." I force my lips into a smile. "What time?"

CHAPTER 12

I open my door at precisely 11:00 a.m. and smile. Max is striding down the hall toward me, a bag slung over his shoulder. Just the familiar sight of him calms my nerves.

"I'm really glad to see you," he says, concern in his eyes.

I step out into the hallway and pull the door closed behind me. "Let's go. I gotta get out of here," I say, pointing to the elevator.

A few minutes later we exit the front and Max slides a glance my way. "I can't believe I let you go out on your own last night with those codes. I'm basically never forgiving myself. When that meeting I was staffing at let out early, I thought for sure you'd been caught. Everyone was on edge."

"Then you don't know?"

Panic fills his face. "Know what?"

Max is already aware of too much for me to hold back on a confession. He'll find out about the break-in eventually. But I don't have to tell him about Javen.

Leaning into Max, I whisper, "They were probably on edge because of me."

His eyes widen. "So, you did go to the Capitol building?"

"I made it inside. But I just got scared and left." I hate lying, but I need to feed him something. "I don't think anyone saw me. Guards entered the building after I'd left. I might have accidentally set off an alarm."

Max sighs. "Well, I'm glad you're safe."

"Me too."

"And you're sure they didn't identify you?"

"If the guards did, I'd think the authorities would already be here."

"Yeah, I suppose that's true." He gestures to his bag. "I brought an early lunch, and there's a park about five blocks from here." My stomach rumbles at the mention of food. I haven't eaten anything since last night at the restaurant. Max eyes me humorously and asks, "Hungry yet?"

"Starving."

The park is small, barely more than a separation between the two buildings flanking it. Especially small compared to the vast forest I was in last night with Javen. Even so, the park has a few trees, green grass, and four stone tables with benches. An Agrowbot buzzes through the space, tending to the plant life.

Max flops his bag onto a table and starts to unload the food, placing two red apples on a plate. The fruit looks suspiciously like the ones we had on the ship before we left. It could be a complete coincidence, but the offering also makes me wonder if Max is perhaps interested in more than just friendship. I mean, what guy pays attention to details—like apple type—unless he likes a girl?

"I wanted to be able to talk with you about the meeting I was working at last night," Max says, pulling me from my thoughts. "The minute I heard what was going on, I knew you'd be interested. Then a call came in, and the meeting broke up quickly. After everyone left, I messaged you but you didn't answer. That's when I started worrying, so I went straight to your dorm."

My mind lights up with the events of last night—how Javen blew out the window, our jump, and how we landed in a river. "Everything was so crazy," I begin. "I finally noticed your message after midnight, but I was so scared from almost getting caught that I forgot to reply."

"I still can't believe you were nearly caught." Max hands me a paper-wrapped sandwich. "I brought turkey and cheese. I hope that's okay."

"It's fine. Thank you." I unwrap the sandwich and bite into it, ignoring the apples. "So, what's your news?"

He leans in closer to me. "You're not going to believe how things are heating up on the Board. With your dad's absence, there's a spot open."

I place my sandwich down on its paper. Every ounce of my hunger dissipates with those words.

"But the Board is divided on who should take the seat," he continues. "Hirata and Cooper made several recommendations of well-respected men and women who worked on your dad's team. But Hammond has rejected every one of their recommendations."

My chest burns with anger. I've met Dad's team, and they're good people who agreed with his vision. No wonder Hammond doesn't want them. "Who does she want?"

"That's the thing. It doesn't make sense."

"Who?" I urge.

Max's lips form a thin line, as if he doesn't want to tell me.

"You're the one who brought the topic up," I say.

"Luca Powell."

"Luca Powell!" I shout and jump to my feet.

"Hey, I was just as shocked as you"—Max's eyes grow wide and he looks around— "but please, sit down."

I drop into my seat and shove the sandwich across the stone tabletop. If I thought my appetite was gone before, now I'm certain hunger will never return.

"Luca Powell can't be older than twenty," I practically snap, my voice low. "And he knows *nothing* about terraforming. Why would Hammond want him on the Board?" And then an idea clicks. This is why she's pulling me in. A sick feeling rounds in my stomach.

"He's nineteen."

I scoff. "Hammond wants a person she can control, making Luca the right guy for the job. You know, he came to my dorm this morning."

Max nearly chokes on his sandwich. "Why?"

"To offer me a job."

"A job?" he asks. "What about the restaurant?"

I lift an eyebrow. "Apparently my terraforming skills aren't being realized there."

Max is silent for a moment. "Hammond wants you to work for the Board so they don't need anyone else on your father's team. You're young . . . controllable."

"Apparently."

Max has completely recovered from choking and proceeds to down the last two bites of his sandwich. "You told him no, right?"

"Actually, I agreed."

"What? Why?"

I take a slow, deep breath and, deciding that I might be able to eat again, pick up my lunch. "Working there gets me inside the building without having to sneak around. On my own, I'm not going to get the information

I need. But working inside the Capitol building? I'll have better access to the people I need to speak with." I take a small bite.

Max grabs one of the apples. "Okay. Well, I can see your point. My guess? Hammond is going to do what she wants when it comes to filling the open seat. So, being on the inside might work." He bites into his apple with a loud crunch and says, mouth full, "Just be careful."

I need a new topic, even if just for a few minutes. "Why'd you come to Arcadia, Max?"

He finishes his bite and sets the fruit down. "My parents paid for my trip."

I look at him, eyes wide, because I fully expected him to say he was trying to claw himself out of a terrible situation on Earth . . . but in essence, he's a patron. Max's family is rich. "Then why are you working?"

Max shrugs. "I want to, like to. And most of the people I work for know me . . . or at least they know my family. Either way, they trust me because of my connection, which keeps me stocked with information." He pauses and lifts a half-smile. "Information is valuable. More valuable than CosmicCoin sometimes."

I shake my head. Max is clever. And the fact that he's only seventeen definitely helps him to fly smoothly under the radar. I lift a half-smile of my own as new questions pop into my head.

"Who's your famil—?" I barely get the question out when, from out of the corner of my eye, I see a figure enter the park. I glance at the person and my stomach does a flip—Javen. He's dressed in simple khaki pants and a gray T-shirt, and his head is down as if he's uncomfortable or trying to avoid notice. He glances up at me for half a heartbeat and then focuses on the grassy earth.

Max turns his head to see where I'm glancing. "What are you staring at?"

"Um . . . oh, I just thought we should be careful what we talk about when other people are here at the park."

He twists around again. "Other people? Uh, we're the only ones here."

Confused, I look to Javen and then to Max. Can't Max see Javen? It seemed as if Alina couldn't see him the other day, either.

"I only meant if more people were here."

Max squints at me and then returns to his apple.

Needing an excuse to speak with Javen, I check my Connect for the time. "Thank you so much for lunch, but—"

Max peers down at my mostly uneaten sandwich. "Not that you ate."

"Too much is going on for me to feel very hungry. Thank you for doing this anyway."

"No problem," Max says.

"I'll message you soon to keep you up to date." I glance at Javen, who's still waiting. "But I have to go now." I wave goodbye to Max and head toward the edge of the park.

"Why are you here?" I whisper to Javen as I reach his side, but I keep my back to Max. "And why can't anyone else see you?"

Javen studies the ground. "That's difficult to explain."

"Well, I'm listening." I look at Max who is staring our direction and then return my gaze back to Javen. "We need to find someplace more out of the way." I wave goodbye to Max, hoping I appear natural.

Not far is an empty walkway, and both Javen and I duck into it. I check the neighboring street, relaxing when it appears we are hidden from view.

"Javen, what's going o—"

Before I have a chance to finish, his hands are in my hair and he's pulling me into his arms. All my questions turn to mush in my brain.

"I had to see you again," he says in a deep voice, deeper than I remember hearing him speak before. "When we touched—in the city, something happened. I saw you. I saw everything about you. It's as if we've always been together."

My knees go weak, and thankfully he continues to hold me or I'm pretty sure I'd find myself on the ground.

"I saw you, too," I say, breathless, and cup my hands over his shoulders to draw him even closer.

He leans down until our noses touch, and before he closes his eyes, I see his dark irises swirl with cyan. Then his soft lips touch mine and my breath hitches in both shock and excitement. Without any hesitation, I sink into the kiss, delirious. The world around us shifts. My mind transports to the blue-green dream world from when I was unconscious on the ship, where I saw him and reached out to him but couldn't connect. His memories, now stored in my mind, flutter through my consciousness. Kissing him makes them feel all the more real. I grip onto his neck, never wanting to let go now that he is here with me. Never wanting our kiss to end.

But a blazing white light ends the vision, and I snap open my eyelids, breathless.

Javen loosens his embrace, though longing remains in his expression.

"How is all this possible," I whisper. "What's happening to us?"

He lets out a long breath. "It's more than that now, but the effect has to do with the Starfire."

I ease from him. "The Starfire? I don't understand."

"Yes, the Starfire has powers. You experienced what the crystal could do. It's bonding us together."

Is this why I've been experiencing all these longings against my better judgment? I shake my head in confusion and then move to lean on the building's metal wall. It's as if an outside force is compelling us together. But something in me doesn't want it to stop. "I still don't understand what's going on."

"When I saved you on the ship, the Starfire connected us. Somehow . . ." He pauses as if he's trying to identify the right words.

My thoughts race far too much to wait for him to finish. "So, is what we're feeling even real?"

Javen stares deep into my eyes and whispers, "More real than anything I've ever known."

Everything in my body longs to fall into his arms again. But I force my mind to remain focused so I can be certain I understand what is going on. I think back to when I was chasing Javen on the street and knew the layout of the building I cut through—a building I had never been in before. "So the Starfire transfers some of your knowledge or memories to me?"

"Yes. Melding our memories. Our life experiences."

I nibble the inside of my bottom lip. "So, why was the Starfire in my dad's jacket?"

He tips his head as if the question catches him off guard. "It was given to him as a gift."

"A gift? By whom?"

"The Council," Javen says.

I have no idea what he's talking about.

Javen leans against the building near me and offers a shy smile. As if sensing my thoughts, he says, "My people live on Arcadia, too."

"Your people?"

He nods. "The Alku. We were here first on Paxon."

I step away from the wall and face him. "Paxon? Arcadia was uninhabited before our ships came."

"I can assure you the Alku were here first. We've lived on Paxon for a very long time. This planet is ours."

I swivel my head to examine my surroundings. "Where are they? The place from last night?"

"That part is difficult to explain. But essentially, we inhabit the same space but in a different plane of existence—"

Is this guy completely crazy?

I take a single step back and dart my eyes around the street.

"—The Starfire is the link between our two worlds. When your kind came and began building, it disturbed the crystal deposits and began to damage the Intersection between the two planes."

There's no way any of this can be true. Questions reel in my mind and anxiety burns in my chest. But I manage to ask, "So, how do you speak English?"

He thinks for a moment. "When your people first interacted with the Starfire, many of Earth's languages were transferred to my people." Javen's face grows sad.

"After the discovery, your father came to the planet. I don't understand all the details. But I do know my people's Council watched him and trusted his judgment. They met with your father, and he tried to inform your World Senate that Primaro would need to be relocated and the Starfire left alone."

"Dad came here? When?"

Javen pauses. "Several years ago. Soon after the work on Primaro had begun."

I think back. The only time Dad went out of town for more than a few days was when he and Mom attended a research conference in Europe. Why would my parents have kept this a secret from me? "Did my mom come, too?"

He shrugs. "She may have, but I only know about your father. I could ask if you'd like."

Tears burn in my eyes. Maybe this is why the planet made Dad feel closer to Mom.

Concern washes over Javen's face. "Have I made you upset?"

I hold my hand up to him and touch his chest. "No, not exactly."

In a flash, he takes me into his warm embrace. "Your father's goal was for my people and yours to live in harmony. But from what I understand, that isn't what's happening. Tension is high among my leaders, and I fear something very dangerous is on the horizon."

A chill runs down my spine. "Could your people have caused the explosion in the bay?"

He pulls my chin up to him. "Your father and his ideals were important to the Council. I had orders to be there to help protect him. And I regret not being able to do more for your family."

"Why do you care about my family so much?"

"The Council trusted your father. They listened to his story of Earth's plight and found it compelling. They wanted to help." He looks away.

For some reason, a sudden heaviness grows in my heart. "What else is there?"

"The Alku believe helping the humans to be a sort of atonement."

"Atonement?"

"We must make up for our past mistakes." Javen steps back and angles slightly from me.

"And is this how you feel, too? As if you need atonement?" I touch my hand to his shoulder and allow my fingers to graze over him. His energy seems to transfer through my skin, making my breath tremble.

"Yes," he whispers. "Sometimes, I do."

CHAPTER 13

My mind blazes with a jumble of thoughts about the Starfire, Javen, and his people. Then how my dad knew everything about Arcadia.

After leaving Javen, I race into the dorm and to my room. I throw open the door, ready to research the Board members I might be able to approach for help.

"What are you in such a hurry about?" Irene asks.

I jump since I thought the place would be empty. "Why are you home and not at work?"

Irene returns to chopping a head of lettuce at the kitchen counter. "My boss sent a bunch of us home early. I have no idea why. But Extra Solar is still working out all the shifts."

I glance at the computer on my desk. But what I want to do will need to wait until I have privacy. I'm not sure how much more I want Irene to get wrapped up into this whole thing. I slip off my shoes and place them to the side of the door.

"Why don't you take a seat? I'm making a late lunch."

"Oh, I ate already." I think back to the few bites I had of the sandwich Max brought.

Irene gives me a once-over. "Sit. You're eating."

"You sure are bossy." I chuckle and walk to the barstool at the kitchenette counter and sit.

"That's what happens when you raise three kids younger than you for six years." She dumps the lettuce into two bowls and moves on to slicing a tomato.

"Three?"

She shrugs. "My cousins. Two girls and a boy. My parents left when I was just a little kid, and my aunt ended up taking me in. But only if I cared for all her kids. I was only nine, but otherwise I'd have been out on the streets."

"Why couldn't your aunt take care of them?"

"She was working. I didn't ask what kept her out so late and she didn't tell me," Irene says as she finishes up the salads and brings our lunch over for us to eat. "She's a good person, though."

"Where'd you live?"

"Los Angeles."

I cringe. I've heard about LA. It's dangerous, and the city's air quality is awful. There are days you can't even leave your home without a respirator. And if the smog doesn't kill you, the people there might.

"I know what you're thinking. How'd a girl from the slums of LA end up working for Extra Solar, right?"

I glance at her as she places a fork next to my bowl.

"Not really. I was thinking about the bad air."

Irene laughs. "The bad air is exactly what got me here."

I tip my head, not understanding.

"I spent so much time indoors that I needed a hobby to not go crazy. So, I turned to computers—games, hacking, and legit stuff too, like school. Pretty soon people online took notice of my skills, and I started picking up odd pro jobs. When the exams came up for a chance to come to Arcadia, I jumped at the opportunity. And only because my identity would be blacked out from the judges until after the scores were in. I guess somebody at the top was valuing skills over breeding—or maybe a few of us were hungrier and willing to leave everything we knew."

"Your cousins?" I pick up my fork and stab at the salad. "Did they come with you?"

"I agreed with my aunt to transfer part of my wages to Earth. It's the same CosmicCoin here as there. In a couple of years, I might be able to get them out of LA." She places a bite of salad in her mouth.

"Do you miss your family?"

"A lot," she mumbles with her mouth full of food and then finishes swallowing. "But what I can make is more than I could swing on Earth, even if most of the funds are to pay off my incurred debt for getting here. My aunt agreed that one of us leaving LA was better than none. Even online, most employers won't pay you as much if they know where you're from."

"Why would it matter if you were the best for the job? How strange."

Irene plops down her fork. "Are you that out of touch, Cassi?"

"Seriously, what do you mean?"

"How much money you have and where you're from matters. If you're from a place like LA, you're going to have a hard time digging your way out, even if you're smart. Even if you're the best at what you do. The rich don't really want people leaving the slums unless it's to their advantage. So, when I found out the testing for traveling to Arcadia only needed my name and that's it, I knew I had the only chance I was going to get. And here I am."

I study her face. Something glinting in Irene's dark eyes reflects a soul who is way beyond her years, and now I understand why. "You're a strong person."

"We all do what we have to do," she says and munches on another bite of salad, and then motions to my food. "Now, are you going to eat that? Don't you waste my money."

I poke the greens with my fork and stuff a bite into my mouth. The salty, sharp taste of the dressing zings across my taste buds. "It's good."

"Thanks. It's my grandmother's salad dressing recipe."

"It's delicious." I take another bite and then another. "What's in it?"

She shakes her head. "Nope . . . family secret. But all this fresh produce available here has me inspired. We didn't get much where I lived, and when we did, I always figured out how to make it taste as good as it could."

"Well, you have a gift," I say and finish up the rest of my salad. Irene finishes her lunch at the same time, so I take our empty bowls to the sink and drop them in. "Speaking of gifts, I need you to help me again. If you're willing, that is."

"What?" she asks.

My request is big, and my chest tingles with anxiety for even thinking to ask. But Irene is right. The people in charge want to maintain power, and they do that by keeping the weak in their place. This whole thing could be so much bigger than I thought, and I might not have time to wait for Hirata and Cooper. "I need someone—you—to hack in and search the video feeds from the day of the explosion on the ship." The words tumble out and I look away, afraid to see her reaction.

"No problem," she says.

"Really?" I swing my attention to her.

"It's going to take a little time. But I can do it. If your dad is still alive, I want to help you find him."

I squeal and then throw my arms around her neck and hug her. She returns the embrace with less enthusiasm and pats me on the shoulder just as both of our devices vibrate simultaneously.

I glance down at the screen as a message appears.

President Hammond will be making an important announcement at 2:00 p.m. Please tune in to the Arcadian Information Feed or gather in the city center to view.

"You want to head down there?" Irene asks.

"No, too crowded and we only have a few minutes. Let's watch the announcement here." I walk from the kitchen and activate the media screen on the wall. The Board's symbol displays.

A light knock echoes from the door.

My breath hitches when the first person I think of is Javen. But I push those thoughts away since there's no way he'd come to my dorm.

"Who is it?" I call.

"Alina," the muffled voice returns.

I look to Irene.

"Well, she knows we're here. So you have to let her in now," she says, and her lips pull into a smile.

I open the door and Alina is standing in the hall, dressed in a coral T-shirt and jeans.

"You going to let me in?" She raises both of her eyebrows.

I gesture Alina in and shut the door.

"Hey, Irene," she says as she steps inside.

"Why aren't you at work?" I ask Alina.

She scowls and flops onto a chair in front of the media screen. "Because I don't have one yet."

"What do you mean?" Irene asks. "A job is required to be here."

"You think I don't know that?" Alina snaps. "The one I had secured was eliminated due to restructuring."

"What about the one you were interviewing for the other day?" I ask.

"Nope, didn't get it," she says. "If I don't secure a position soon, I don't know what's going to happen. There's no way I can live in the dorm if I don't have a job. Eventually, they will detain me."

"Even if you're actively searching?" I ask.

"I think we have two weeks," Irene says.

"There's a server position open at Spectra," I say. "I just got a new position at the Capitol building."

"Server?" Alina throws her hands into the air. "I didn't get a top score on my executive assistant exams to come here and serve people food."

"What?" Irene asks me, ignoring Alina's outburst. "You didn't tell me this."

"It happened this morning. Sorry. But I'm not that thrilled about the job."

Alina scoffs. "You go from working as a server in a restaurant to a job with the Board, and you're not that thrilled about it? What's wrong with you?"

My chest tightens at her words. Alina still doesn't know what is going on with me. "It's just . . . my dad was caught up in the ship explosion, and the Board wants me to take over part of what he was doing."

Alina's eyes widen. "Richard Foster? You're his daughter?"

"Cassi is short for Cassiopeia," Irene says and shoots me a warning glare.

"Oh, wow," Alina says. "I didn't know."

"I didn't tell you." I pull up a desk chair beside Alina and Irene sits in the other living area seat.

On the screen, the Board symbol disappears and we quiet. A camera pans over the Board members, who appear to be indoors while an orchestral piece plays, I suppose to inspire us all to greatness.

I'm not very familiar with all of the members, but Hammond is of course there. And I spot Lawrence Cooper and Lia Hirata, the two I need to contact. Hirata is the youngest member, probably in her early forties, Asian descent, and with long, straight black hair that hangs down her back. She sits with her hands folded in her lap, but her jaw is tense. Hirata throws a look at Cooper, who returns the gaze, raises an eyebrow to her, and then releases a long breath. Cooper has dark skin, ultra-short hair, and is somewhere around my dad's age.

To Hammond's left is Enzo Leon. His wavy, dark hair is graying at the temples, and from the times I've heard Dad mention him, Leon is Hammond's puppet. A smug smile makes its home on his lips. There are two others, both women I know little about, but I intend to soon.

Hammond stands, and the Board members look to her.

"Greetings Arcadians," she says, staring into the camera. Her white, shoulder-length hair frames her sharp features.

I wonder if she's speaking to us or the people who lived on this planet first?

"I called you here today because I have important news that is about to change our lives further," Hammond continues. "As details play out, we continue to restructure companies and available jobs. I know many of you are worried after the unanticipated changes since we arrived on Arcadia. But it is my goal that each of you will find your place among us on this new journey.

The Board has decided to extend the deadline to secure a job, and if one is not found by that time, those who are still unemployed will be offered a temporary position."

I glance at Alina as she swings her legs to the floor and sits taller in her seat.

"When the initial scouts came to Arcadia, we knew the ground was full of vast riches, including mineral deposits and precious metals. But what we continue to discover amazes us more each day. We have discovered an ore the Board believes will change our very existence."

Electricity races through my veins. Hammond can't be talking about the Starfire. I lean toward the screen and wipe my sweaty palms across my skirt.

"Additional ships are arriving from Earth over the next week with thousands of new passengers to start up a mining colony. We will also be amping up building production in the city, which will create an opportunity for more jobs as well as bring tens of thousands more people from Earth well ahead of schedule."

Hammond pauses, and a crowd of journalists in front of her erupts with questions.

"What is this new ore?" one shouts.

"Will this discovery bring new tech jobs to the city?" another calls out.

Hammond raises her hands to quiet their questions. "I won't be answering any questions. But my—*our*—

vision of the project is evolving. The Board is prepared to feed new information to the public, as necessary."

The crowd of reporters breaks into shouts again.

"I will not be answering questions," she insists. "But I will announce that we have a new Board member." She gestures to the side, and the camera pans back. Luca emerges.

"Luca Powell may be young, but he has incredible ideas about our rising future," she says as Luca joins her at her side.

I knew this was going to happen, but seeing him makes my teeth grit. I shoot to my feet and shout at the screen, "Why is she doing all this?"

"What's wrong with you?" Alina says. "It's all amazing news."

I swing around to Alina and then flick my attention to Irene. "I need air." I grab for my shoes next to the door and slip them on. Then I throw open the door and march out.

"I don't get it," Alina says.

"She's just emotional. A lot has happened in the last week," Irene says before the door slams shut. I want to be angry at her, too. But I know she's only covering for me.

I race from the dorm to a mostly empty street, fury burning in my chest. Hammond has to be aware of Javen's people, and if the Alku own the Starfire, we can't just take it. The people must know what is going on. I speed to the Capitol building to locate anyone who will listen.

Out of nowhere, a dark figure appears on the sidewalk, and I slam into their frame. I step back. "I'm so sorry." Rubbing my chest, I look up to Javen.

"What are you doing here?" I ask.

"Stopping you."

"Stopping me, why? Someone has to do something."

An expression of worry washes over his face, and Javen motions me away from the middle of the sidewalk. I follow his cue since I keep forgetting that no one else can see him.

"How do you know where I'm going, anyway?" I ask.

"I'm not sure. A few minutes ago, I was drawn to your Starfire, and I knew you planned to tell people about us. It's the effect of the crystal." Javen takes my shoulders. "You can't do this."

"Why? Someone has to."

"Someone did. Or at least attempted to."

I move from his touch. "Then take me to them. Maybe they can help me."

Javen's expression grows sad. "I can't. That person was your father."

I narrow my eyes at him. "My dad obviously wanted to work with you."

He shakes his head. "I know, but making the knowledge of my people public is a mistake. One that could get you killed."

I know he's right and I need more time to make a plan.

"Fine. But I won't let my parents' vision be destroyed." I turn from him and walk away.

CHAPTER 14

Part of me wants Javen to follow me, but the other part wants to be alone. I glance around, and he's gone. His absence steals the breath from my lungs for a moment.

I graze the ring on my finger. *What do I do, Mom?* I listen for any kind of response, but nothing comes.

As I walk, a few pedestrians move from the buildings onto the street. Hammond's announcement must be over. I walk the streets until I identify the park Max took me to and plop onto the nearest bench. I study one of the trees and notice a blue bird building a nest in the highest branches, one I'm completely unfamiliar with, sporting a long-feathered tail.

I have no idea what kind of bird it is; I'm sure a native species of this planet. Maybe it's an Arcadia pigeon. If so, they're a lot prettier than Earth pigeons. My shoulders droop a notch. The bird weaves a few twigs into her project, just as any mother bird would do on Earth. Strange how I'm so far away from home, but essentially life here is the same.

I gaze at Mom's ring, and my lips stretch into a sad smile. I'd better get back.

I open the door to my room and find Irene alone and lounging on her bed with a DataPort perched on her lap.

"Alina left?"

"Finally," she mumbles without looking from the display while continuing to type. "That girl talks and talks and talks."

I flop into a chair and spin the seat around to face her. "She say anything else about me after I left?"

Irene stops typing and glances up. "Be careful around people. I've seen enough that you can't be too careful about who you can trust."

"Worked out okay with you."

She clicks her tongue. "That could've turned out bad, too." Irene turns the computer screen toward me. "I'm progressing with hacking into the ship's feed."

"How long do you think it'll take?"

"I'm not sure. Maybe by tomorrow."

I move from the chair to her bunk and sit. "How do you do it?"

"Hacking?"

"Yeah." I peer at the screen, and it looks like nothing but a bunch of garbled symbols.

Irene laughs. "It's not a skill I could teach you in a few hours."

"I know. But I'm a fast learner."

Irene nods and runs me through the program she's using. Admittedly, I don't understand half of it, but a few of the steps and terms make sense.

"So, you think you know enough for a job at Extra Solar now?" she teases.

I let out a chuckle. "If only. The day after tomorrow I'm going to start my job at the Capitol building."

Irene closes the lid to her DataPort. "How did that happen? I mean, it's good, right? It gets you inside, at least."

"That's exactly why I took it. Between you and me, we should have information on my dad soon. I have no idea what we'll do with it. But I'll think of something. If we get hard evidence, someone will listen, right?"

Irene shrugs. "I hope so."

My Connect buzzes with a message from Max.

Meet me downstairs. I have good news.

"Max wants to meet me," I say and scoot off the bunk.

"I'll be here." Irene returns to working on her DataPort.

"See you later." I hurry out the door and downstairs to see what news he has.

When Max sees me, he smiles. "Come with me. I have a person for you to meet. I was able to get a permanent hire with one of the Board members."

I follow his lead. "Who?"

"Lia Hirata," he says. "I was assigned to a position on her security team."

"How'd you swing a job like that? Your parents?"

"No. The last guy I was working for is a sympathizer with a lot of pull. He doesn't agree with Hammond. The two of us have spent a lot of time together over the last few days, and I've expressed a few concerns about the secrecy of the explosion, how everything looks like it was swept under the rug. I knew he was close to Hirata, so I asked for him to put in a good word. Two hours ago, he messaged that she was increasing her security team."

"Right after the announcement?"

"Pretty much," he says. "She wanted to meet with me right away, and I didn't hold back. I told her about what's going on with you and that you needed help."

My breathing picks up, and my thoughts turn to my conversation with Javen. If I speak to Hirata, I'm only going to keep to the explosion and my dad. I told Javen I wouldn't bring up his people. And I have no idea how much Hirata knows when it comes to co-inhabiting Arcadia anyway. One thing at a time. But if she can help me with Dad, I can trust her with the rest.

"Let's go meet her."

Max and I hurry the rest of the way to the Capitol building. As I study the large structure the next block over, my stomach drops. What if Hammond sees me here?

"You don't need to worry," Max says as if he's read my mind. "Hammond gave you a free pass into the building by hiring you. I had Hirata add you to the security list early. Anyway, Hammond left after the announcement. Probably to avoid questions."

His words don't help my churning stomach, but I keep my feet moving forward. We pass through the security checkpoint easily, then use the elevator to the twentieth floor where Hirata's office is located. Once there, Max palms the security pad on the side of the door.

With her back to us, Hirata gazes out a large picture window. She turns as we step in, her arms crossed over her chest and worry seeped into her expression—until she recognizes Max. Relieved, she uncrosses her arms and makes a beeline toward us, extending her hand.

"I'm so sorry for all you've been through." She takes my hand and squeezes my palm tightly.

I realize, as her words comfort the ache in my heart, that she's the first adult since the accident who has said anything like this to me. A wave of emotion overtakes my body.

"Thank you," I say, clutching her hand. "You don't know how much that means to me. Do . . . do you know what happened in the explosion, to my dad?"

Hirata releases my hand and gestures Max and me toward two chairs in front of her desk. We each take a seat, and she rounds the desk to her chair.

"I wish I knew more, but Hammond isn't releasing information from the investigation. The residents of Primaro have already accepted the incident as just a horrible accident. Publicly closing the case made it easier for everyone to move on with their new lives." Hirata taps the top of her desk and a hologram of a building appears. "What I do know is that your belongings are being held in here." She points to the building.

"How will I be able to get in?" I ask.

"That's the strange thing," Hirata says. "The boxes were sent to public storage and haven't even been pulled yet for the investigation. But anyone can enter the facility."

"What about the code?" Max asks.

"I have it." Hirata pulls open her desk drawer and reaches in. She hands me a slip of paper with the building's address and a set of numbers on it.

25504
4508129543

I study the numbers and stuff the paper in my pocket.

"The first is the storage room and the second is the code to open it," she says.

My heart picks up its pace. "And you think there might be something in there that can help me?"

Hirata lifts a delicate shoulder in a slight shrug. "To be honest . . . I don't know, Cassi. But it's the best I can do right now. Hammond shouldn't be keeping your father's things from you."

Frustration brews in my chest. Hirata must be aware of more than she's telling us. "You're on the Board. Why don't you use your influence to do more than get me the code and location of my dad's possessions?"

"She's only trying to help." Max's eyes narrow in confusion. "We have to start somewhere."

I stand and stare at her. "No. This is so much bigger than you're admitting. My dad knew about the Starfire, and you know about it too."

Hirata's eyes grow wide. "How do you know about the Starfire? That word is classified."

"Starfire?" Max asks.

Hirata stands and moves her gaze between Max and me. She looks down and taps away at the hologram. "I'm on your side, Cassi. But the Starfire is not a topic I'm able to discuss with you right now. I suggest you forget this . . . information . . . and go check your father's items for anything sentimental. If I learn anything concerning the investigation, I will let you know."

"You know this whole situation needs more thought on your part," I say.

She tips her head, and her tense expression softens. "Of course I do. But if I make waves before I have the evidence I need, there might be another unexplained explosion."

Her words punch me in the stomach, and I gape at her.

"Max," she says. "I'd like you to escort Miss Foster to the storage facility and then return when you've seen her safely home."

Max stands. "Yes, ma'am." He eyes me and I gesture with my head to the door.

"Please think about what I said," I say to Hirata before we exit.

"I hope you locate what you need in your father's belongings," she responds.

I push out of the office, clenching my teeth.

"What were you talking about in there?" Max whispers, leaning into me. "Starfire? I thought we were here to talk about your dad?"

"Cassi, Max." A female voice comes from behind, and I swing toward the source.

Alina walks toward us, all smiles and dressed in a pair of blue pants and an aqua shirt.

"Why are you in the Capitol building?" I ask, hoping she didn't overhear anything Max had just spoken to me.

Alina looks from me to Max, lingering a second too long on him. She clears her throat. "I had a job interview."

"You did? What position?" I ask.

She looks away. "It's not great . . . probably the assistant to an assistant. I'm sure I'll end up getting coffee for everyone if I get the position."

"But it's something, right?" I say, trying to stay positive for her but, all the while, itching to get out of here.

"Exactly," she says.

"Sorry, Alina," Max interrupts. "But Cassi and I have to go."

Alina smiles at him. "No, problem. Maybe I can see you later?"

"Maybe," I say and pull Max's arm. But I'm fully aware she's not talking to me. "Good luck with the job."

Max follows my lead and we hustle to the elevator.

"Bye," Alina says from behind.

Max and I step out onto the ground floor and walk to the street.

"Can you tell me what happened back there?" Max asks.

I rub my temple. I don't really know what's going on anymore. Everything I could tell Max sounds completely crazy. People are living on this planet no one can see but me. And magic crystals have to do with all of this . . . weirdness. He'll think that I'm experiencing a mental breakdown or something. I swallow back the fear and consider my friend.

"I'm not sure," I answer quietly. "All I know is Hammond's announcement means something bad is going to happen on Arcadia. And my dad knew about it."

"And what's this word 'Starfire?'"

"I must have heard my dad say the word one time." I place my hand in my pocket and pull out the paper Hirata gave me. "Let's go to the storage unit."

Max doesn't say anything for a few seconds. I'm sure he knows that I'm avoiding his question. "I recognized the building on the hologram. It's about eight blocks from here. You want to walk or grab a ride?"

My body radiates with nervous energy. "Walking is probably best."

About thirty minutes later, we arrive at the facility. The front doors slam behind us and echo in the cement space. I glance around the long gray hallway lined with wide metal doors. The place is empty.

"What's the unit again?" Max asks.

I uncrumple the paper from my hand. "25504."

He scans the directory. "That's on the second floor."

Max and I take the stairs to the second floor and locate the unit. I enter the code, and as I open the door, an automatic light comes on overhead. Inside, at least twenty-five storage boxes crowd the unit, stacked several high. None of them are labeled.

"Well, one at a time," Max says.

I tip my head. "I guess I don't have anything to do until tonight."

My stomach sinks when I remember how I'm supposed to eat dinner with Luca to discuss my new job.

"You start on the right, and I'll start on the left," he says.

"Okay." I walk to the nearest box and open the lid. Inside are items I recognize from our home on Earth. Another time, I'd probably be happy to see them. But this isn't a time for keepsakes.

I dig through the box and several others, finding nothing to help me. Max's boxes are no better. I do spot my missing items, but to be honest, I haven't needed anything and there's no room in the dorm, so I might as well leave everything here.

"This is useless," I say, plopping onto the cold ground. "These are all just personal items."

"There's still a bunch more." Max lifts the top off a new box and rifles through the contents. He lifts out a smaller container and opens the top. "Your dad went to Europe? Did you go too?"

My ears perk up at his words, and I spring to my feet. "No, what did you find?"

"Souvenirs?" He shrugs and pulls an item out. "And I think this is a thumb drive. It's pretty old tech. I haven't seen one in a long time."

I snatch the device from his hand. "We need to get this to Irene."

Max tips his head in confusion. "Now your dad's vacation pictures suddenly interest you?"

"My parents never went to Europe. They came to Arcadia."

CHAPTER 15

Max and I burst through the door to my room, and Irene slams shut the lid to her computer.

She exhales, relieved. "It's you two. Alina has been by here two times while you were gone."

I close the door. "We found something . . . I might need your help." My breath comes out in pants as I hold the thumb drive out to her.

Irene puts aside the computer and stands. She walks to us and glances from my hand to Max and back at my palm. "I haven't seen one of those in a long time. I can't access the data here, though. I'm going to need specialized equipment. What do you think is on it?"

"It could be nothing," I say, my breathing finally returning to normal. "But I got access to my dad's missing stuff, and this was in it."

"And you think what's on the drive has to do with the explosion?"

I shake my head.

"Cassi's parents came here on a secret trip," Max blurts out. "The drive might tell us why." His Connect buzzes, and he lifts his wrist to look at it. His shoulders sink. "Hirata needs me at the office." He looks to me. "You let me know if you find anything."

"We will," I say.

"I'll message you when I get off work," Max says as he slips out the door.

I nod, but I doubt he sees me. "So, how is the progress with the ship's feeds?" I ask Irene.

"Good," she says. "I thought it would take me longer. But I'm nearly in. I should have access by tonight." She walks to the bowl of fruit in the kitchen and grabs a plum. "How soon do you need whatever is on this thumb drive?"

I press my lips together. I need all of it *now*. "As soon as you can."

Irene takes a bite of her plum and peers away as if she's in thought. "I'd like a break anyway. I can head to work and use equipment there to transfer the files to my DataPort."

My Connect buzzes.

Reminder: Dinner with Luca Powell at 5:30 PM

My heart sinks at the sight of the words. It's the last thing I want to do.

Irene leans into me and glances at my wrist. "You're having dinner with Luca Powell?"

"It's not a good thing," I scoff.

"Oh . . . I knew that guy was a slime ball the minute I saw him. But you're the one who wants information, and he might have it if you play your cards right."

I wrinkle my nose and sit on the barstool in the kitchen. "That's the whole reason I even agreed. Our dinner is to discuss my new job."

Irene takes another bite of her plum and raises an eyebrow. "He didn't need to ask for a dinner date to talk about your job, though."

"Like you said, he's a slime ball. I'll be careful."

Irene finishes her plum and tosses the pit into the composter. "I might not be back by the time you leave. Message me if there are any problems."

"Sure thing," I say.

She grabs her DataPort and heads out the door.

Five-fifteen comes too soon, and I'm dressed in a floaty yellow dress with cap sleeves. I hate dressing up for Luca, but I need to play the part. A pit forms in my stomach when I think of the last time I met Javen. I was angry at him for not wanting me to tell anyone about the Alku. I still think it's the only way to stop Hammond from mining the Starfire before we know how it will affect Arcadia.

I straighten the chain of my necklace and fasten one more button on my dress to ensure the crystal stays hidden under the fabric.

I message Irene.

I'm heading out.

But nothing comes back. She must be busy.

With a sigh, I head for the door and make my way down to the street. I search everywhere for Javen. I want to tell him I'm not really interested in having dinner with *Luca*. What if Javen thinks I was so angry at him that I'm doing this to spite him? I shake the silly thoughts from my head. I've barely known Javen a week, and strangely, there's a part of me that's not even sure if he's real. But my mind returns to the kiss we shared. That felt real. More real than anything. The feeling of his mouth on my mine and his incredibly strong arms wrapping around my body . . . my cheeks flush, and heat spreads to my chest.

I look up and Spectra is right in front of me, and the sight jolts me back to my appointment. I gulp in a breath of air and enter the front door. Inside is Suzanna, the manager. Her eyes brighten when she sees me.

"I heard you were promoted," she says.

A weak smile stretches across my lips, and I gather up as much fake excitement as I can. "It was fun working here, but duty calls."

"Yeah," Suzanna says. "You'll be set." She glances down at the computer screen on the hostess station. "Luca Powell is already waiting for you. He reserved the entire back room."

My heartbeat skips with anxiety. I don't want a private room. I force another smile. "Sounds good. Lead the way."

Suzanna steps in front of me and walks toward the rear of the restaurant. On the way, we pass several couples and groups who are already enjoying their dinners. She opens the door to the farthest room, where Luca sits at a solitary round table, studying a menu.

As we enter, he looks up and smiles. Luca is a handsome young man, but something in his expression sends a shiver down my spine, and suddenly I wish I'd brought my sweater.

Luca places his menu down on the table and stands. "Hello, Cassi."

"Hello, Mr. Powell."

He frowns as he pulls out a chair, positioned a bit too close to his for my taste. But I sit anyway. Suzanna leaves and the door shuts behind her.

"I had hoped we might be beyond such formalities by this time." He lowers himself into his seat and leans his elbows on the table. "I'd like it if you called me Luca."

Inside I'm frowning, but I can't let the expression get comfortable on my face. If Luca thinks I don't like him, I'm never going to get anywhere.

A sweet smile overtakes my lips instead. "I'm sorry . . . Luca. I'm very nervous."

Luca returns the smile. "Nervous? There's nothing to be nervous about." He gestures to the menu. "We're only having dinner."

"And discussing my new job."

He waves his hand in the air. "Oh, that. Just a little business before pleasure."

My stomach sinks at the word "pleasure," but I try to hide my distaste by letting a chuckle escape my lips. "So, at the Gala, you mentioned that you don't have any family on Arcadia."

Luca smiles. "You have a good memory. I don't have family here, that's correct. Unlike me, they don't have a lot of ambition. But I always have. When I was thirteen, I took an unpaid training program offered by the World Senate in D.C."

"Washington?"

"Yes, that's where I'm from. My scores in school qualified me for the position and all of my teachers recommended me."

"Your parents must have been proud," I say.

"Not really." A muscle in his jaw twitches. "They hate the World Senate and wanted me to keep my nose out of things. So, I ended up forging their permission slip and doing it anyway."

"Didn't they know you were gone every day?"

Luca shrugs. "They barely noticed when I was there, let alone when I wasn't." Sadness darkens his eyes and I start to feel a twinge of pity for him, until I remember who I'm talking to. "Anyway," he says, "I did that every year until the end of high school. That's how I met Hammond. Instead of college, I was hired straight onto her staff."

"Lucky you." I don't really want to dig into Luca's life, so I change the subject. "How about you tell me what I should expect in the morning?"

Luca pauses as if he's thinking for a moment. "Well, you'll receive a tour of the building first. That way you know where you're going."

"Of course." I lean in and place my elbows on the table to show him my intense interest.

"Then you'll be escorted to your new office—"

"I'm getting an office to myself?"

He nods. "Yeah. Your job requires clearance with the Board, so you'll need a measure of privacy. Then Hammond will probably speak to you about the current project."

"The mining project?" My muscles tense at my words.

"Yes. There are several details we've not been able to resolve. The Board needs an expert to come in and modify the existing terraforming plan."

"And I'm an expert?" I lean back in my seat.

"I've not seen your simulation records. But Hammond seems to think so. I do think you should come prepared though. She's having you dive right into work. No honeymoon period."

I'm not here to talk about me, so I grin at Luca and formulate a way to steer our conversation's focus back onto him.

"So . . . can you believe your luck with being placed on the Board?"

He chuckles. "Luck had nothing to do with it. I've worked very hard to secure President Hammond's trust over the last year."

"What do you know about the mining? Will this new ore really change our lives?" I lean into him again and place my hands on the table.

The door to our private room swings open and an unknown server appears in the opening.

Luca holds up his hand to him. "We'll be ready to order in a few minutes."

The server nods and returns the way he came. The door shuts behind him, and reluctantly I return my attention to Luca.

He raises his hand onto the tabletop, placing his fingers over mine. A nervous jolt travels through my stomach, and everything in me wants to pull from him. But I resist. I need to stay focused on why I'm here: information.

"You were about to discuss the new ore?" I prompt.

His lips curve into a hint of a smile. "No. I don't know much yet. She and I have a meeting tonight after this dinner. But I'm sure Hammond will fill you in as much as you need tomorrow." Luca leans toward me, considerably closer than comfortable. "But I can tell you it's something big, and I'm thrilled both of us are a part of it."

I stare at him, not moving. Unexpectedly, Luca reaches his hand into my hair and bends closer toward me. My heart jumps. He's trying to kiss me!

But before Luca gets that far, a cyan glow appears between us. Cold overtakes my body. Luca's eyes grow wide as he jolts his hand back from me, as if shocked by electricity.

"What was that?" he asks, eyes still wide with shock.

I jump to my feet. "Uh . . . I don't know. I'm going to go ask Suzanna if anything is going on outside."

"No, don't do that."

"It's fine; I'm feeling a little sick, too," I say as Luca's voice is already behind me. I dash for the door and throw it open. As I step through, a hand grips my arm. I gasp and swing around, expecting Luca. But instead, the scene shifts and bends and my surroundings change from the restaurant to a heavily wooded forest.

I swing my head around, and a pair of strong arms pulls me into a safe embrace.

"I've got you," Javen says, and I sink into his chest.

CHAPTER 16

Although I have no desire to, I pull from Javen's embrace. My heart is still racing at the thought of Luca trying to touch me—kiss me.

"How did I get here?" I look up at him. "Was that you who made the Starfire glow? To keep Luca away from me?"

"Luca? The new member of the Board?" Javen's hands form into tight fists and a vein forms on his neck. "What was he doing to you?"

My pulse batters at my eardrums. If Javen doesn't know Luca tried to kiss me, I'm not sure telling him is a good idea. And I want to forget the whole thing happened anyway. "I was meeting with him to talk about my new job, which starts tomorrow. But mostly I was there to try and get information about my dad and maybe the new mining project."

Javen's face softens. "It's dangerous for you to be seeking out information like this. I should never have taken you into Hammond's office. You're going to get yourself hurt."

"I have to know what happened in the explosion. I can't move on if I don't," I say. "But did you bring me here?"

Javen shakes his head. "I didn't do anything. I was out in the woods alone, and then suddenly you were here, but . . ." He pauses. "But not fully. You were transparent. I reached out and then you were solid and in my arms."

I glance around at my location. It appears very much like the place Javen brought me to the first time I was here, except no river. Still no signs of civilization: no other people, no city skyline in the distance, no buildings or structures. Above is only the setting sun. Arcadia's two large moons hang in the night sky, out of sight, and wait to make their appearance. I can make out what might be a few dots of bright stars in the distance.

"So, you didn't use the Starfire to bring me across the Intersection?"

"No, you must have crossed yourself." He turns and rakes his fingers through his thick, dark hair. "I've not seen an Earthling be able to complete the transfer alone. As far as I know, only my people can because of our link to the Starfire." Javen twists my way and runs his hand over his face, revealing a tense jaw.

His gesture sends a sick feeling into my stomach. "I don't understand. Is this a bad thing?"

"I'm not sure what your crossing the Intersection on your own means at this point, but I'm concerned how my people will take the news. It could change things."

"For good?" From his expression the question is a long shot, but I have to ask.

"I'm afraid not." Javen lowers himself to sit on the ground. "The girl who attacked you the other day . . ."

I sit beside him. "How could I forget?" The ghost of her fingers encircling my throat hovers around my skin again, and I reach to touch the spot.

"Her name is Beda, and she's my cousin. The man she was with is my uncle Wirrin."

Cousin? That's why she reminded me of Javen. "Why would your cousin try to strangle me?"

"My people are peaceful. We've always had everything we needed on this planet. The Starfire is a clean energy source and allows us to travel long distances without things like the trains and vehicles you've brought here. We do not need large buildings, either. My people learned to live in nature without giant structures. We can even travel to your dimension for short periods of time. But most of us found little reason to do so. Until humans came from Earth, we had known very little division. However, when your people arrived, their presence created a disturbance."

"A disturbance?"

"Some of the Alku wanted to go back to the old ways. The ways that embraced war."

"But most don't?"

"No," he says.

"And what about you?" I stare at the angles of his face.

Javen's lips curl into a soft smile. "I don't agree with everything the Council decrees, but in this, they are right. The Alku have thrived since we became peaceful, and killing is wrong. I don't want to return to those ways. Your father was working to repair the problem. The city of Primaro was originally much closer to the Starfire fields. He moved the city as far away as he could and was arranging for safeguards to keep the fields undisturbed. It was a good solution and allowed us to share the planet with Earth."

"Then the explosion happened and Dad . . ." Emotion wells in my chest and I can't hold my words back anymore. "Oh, Javen . . . I want to believe my dad is only missing . . . but he's dead, isn't he?"

As fast as the words empty from my mouth, Javen folds me into his arms. "I don't know, Cassi," he whispers into my hair, his voice like music again. "He could still be alive. I don't want to give you false hope.

But you called on the Starfire and the energy bringing you to this side of the Intersection makes the impossible possible."

I lay my head on Javen's chest and breathe in his scent—a fusion between earth and sky, intoxicating my mind and body. Dissolving every thought save thoughts of him. Desire takes over, especially desire for my pain to dissipate, and I snake my hands around his neck while raising my mouth to meet his soft lips.

Javen's feelings are obviously the same for me because he doesn't resist. Not even for a second. He wraps his arms around my waist, and then his hands travel up my spine and to my shoulder blades, entwining our bodies closer.

Our kiss is hungry, though not rushed as his soft lips press into mine. So many times. I run my hands through the base of his hair and don't let him go. My body fills with warmth and excitement, feelings that consume me as my hands roam to his shoulders. I want this moment to last forever. Wonder fills me, and when I crack open my eyelids to peek at him, we're both enveloped in a cyan glow. At the sight, I pull from his lips.

"Please . . . don't stop. Stay with me forever," Javen whispers and opens his eyes, which swirl with color. Then, as if the color were mere mist, the hue dissipates.

He pants for breath but doesn't loosen his hold on my back.

"Is that normal?" I ask, knowing so little about his people. To be honest, I'm not even sure the Alku are human.

Javen lifts a side of his mouth, as if shy. The look is utterly boyish and my pulse glitters in response. "No," he says softly, "but I don't think anything about us is normal."

I've kissed a few boys in the past, even thought I was in love once. But Javen is different. I'm not sure I can determine *exactly* what my feelings for him mean. Though much of me thinks he was right that the Starfire linked us. My heart is bound to his, I realize. And a smile flits across my lips when I also realize I don't want it any other way.

I draw in a steady breath and pull him close to me again, eager to fulfill his request to continue where we left off. Javen's lips part and his hands tighten on my shoulder blades as he lowers to me. But before my lids shut, the world around us shifts. The dirt and trees bend and fade to become buildings and pavement.

My breath hitches as I wonder if we're simply going to appear in each other's arms on the streets of Primaro for anyone walking by to see.

"Are you able to stop it?" I ask as the scene before us seems to pulse.

Javen closes his eyes, inhales a shaky breath, and then opens them again. "I can't control the Starfire this time."

I grab for the necklace under my shirt. "What if I took it off?"

He pulls my hand away. "No, we have no way of knowing if removing the Starfire could damage this Intersection point. I'll do my best to cloak us, though."

I stand, and Javen follows. The pulse stops and the two of us end up on my side of the Intersection. All around us is a light cyan glow. Several people walk by and pay us no mind.

To our left is the restaurant. The front door opens and Luca walks out. Upon seeing him, the memory of his attempt at kissing me floods back and my heart shudders. Apparently, he must not have eaten dinner, not that I blame him after what happened.

Javen's attention swings to Luca. "He didn't harm you, did he?"

I study my feet and lift my shoulders and say, "No." Everything in me wants to leave and return to the dorm. But when I look up at Luca again, an idea forms. "We are invisible, right?"

"Yes. With the Starfire, I can cloak us to be unseen. You are the only person I'm aware of who can see through this cloaking."

"We need to follow Luca," I say. "He told me that he had scheduled a meeting with Hammond tonight after our dinner. They might discuss my dad."

Two lines form between Javen's brows. "I don't want to put you in danger."

I place my hands on his upper arms and gently squeeze. "Javen, you know I can't let my dad go."

Javen sighs and nods. "I'll help you."

I stretch up and give him a quick kiss and release his arms. "Thank you." Then I swing around to Luca, who's already halfway down the block toward the Capitol building.

The two of us sprint after him, and the sensation of moving through the air is exactly how I visualized Javen when I first noticed him in the ship's bay while he was running through the crowd—like he was swimming. Our movements feel as if we are gliding through water, but with little resistance. I can see everything going on around me, but I'm not a part of any of it.

We eventually catch up to Luca and follow him all the way to the Capitol building. Luca makes his way through the front and into the elevator. Javen and I slip in from behind and stand on the opposite side of the cab from Luca.

Unaware of our presence, he chooses the floor and the doors slide shut. My stomach drops as I study his face.

His jaw is tense, and he shoves his hands into his pockets.

Javen stares at Luca, eyes narrowed, and I'm pretty confident that Javen knows I wasn't telling the full truth about my time with Luca. I slip my hand into his to calm him, and luckily Hammond's office is only on the fifth floor, so the ride isn't long.

When the doors slide away, I don't hear the chime. Luca moves out, and we continue to trail him to Hammond's office, just past the briefing room.

"Come in," echoes Hammond's voice from the other side, following Luca's knock.

I gulp down my nervousness as Luca steps into the office. Javen and I rush after him before the doors shut automatically. I tap my Connect and scroll through the options, activate the camera, and hit record. I have no idea what Hammond is going to say, but I might need the footage later.

"Give me just a moment, Luca." Hammond doesn't even look up from her touchscreen. She slides her hand across the surface, studying information.

"Yes, ma'am." Luca folds his hands behind his back.

I tug Javen around to Hammond's side of the screen.

A side-by-side simulation of both Earth and Arcadia displays on the screen. Hammond taps the Earth side, and a countdown begins.

"Come see," she says and waves Luca over.

It's not necessary, but Javen and I step back and allow him to come to her side.

"What is this?" Luca asks.

"Just wait," Hammond says as the counter makes its way to zero.

When zero hits, the Earth side comes to life, spinning on its axis.

"This is a simulation to display the next five years on Earth," she says.

We all watch as the oceans rise and consume more land until the continents shrink.

"Earth has reached the global warming tipping point much faster than anyone expected," Hammond says. "Crop diseases will spring up from the shifts in climate, and mass famine will consume the people as a result."

"I thought the estimates were at least one hundred years out?" Luca says.

Hammond arches an eyebrow. "That's what we want people to believe to prevent mass panic and to retain the hope that Arcadia would be a viable option. But five years doesn't give us enough time. Of course, a percentage will be able to cross the universe and help expand our colony, but the cost will be too exorbitant for most people on Earth to journey here."

Luca tips his head. "So, everyone will die?"

To the side of the Earth's simulation, the death toll grows higher and higher as time goes on. My heart clenches with this information.

"The World Senate is trying to create options. And when Richard Foster discovered the Starfire ore—"

"Starfire?" Luca asks.

I dig my fingernails into my palms at the mention of Dad's name.

"Yes. We knew the ore was special right away, but we were shocked by just how. The Starfire has planet-equalizing properties."

"As in healing?" Luca asks.

"That is our hope. The Senate pushed to start mining right way, and the best scientists were tasked with studying the ore's properties. We needed to discover if bringing the crystals back would stabilize or even rejuvenate Earth's atmosphere and surface."

Luca crosses his arms over his chest. "And *this* is why we're mining it."

Hammond tips her head. "We've found a better use, a faster one. When Foster discovered the Starfire, he discovered something else too."

Luca angles his head in curiosity and my breath quickens in anticipation of her words.

"There are others who inhabit Arcadia."

"What?" Luca asks, his eyes widening. "Where?"

Hammond gestures to the other side of her desk. "You might want to sit down."

Luca obeys.

"The Starfire creates a"—she pauses as if in thought—"a rift of sorts called the Intersection. Foster told the Board about the phenomenon a year after he'd discovered the ore. On one side of the Intersection is us—the Arcadia we know. On the other is an alternate Arcadia—Paxon. A small population of people called the Alku live there."

Luca doesn't say anything and simply stares at Hammond, stunned.

"Our scientists have discovered that, if we take a large amount of the Starfire back to Earth, we can open an Intersection there—a rift to a new world. They've done multiple experiments and it works. We believe a completely untainted world exists on the Intersection's other side on Earth. If we get enough Starfire there, we can use the crystals to open large rifts for many of Earth's inhabitants to cross through much easier than bringing people here. And then we can maintain control of two planets instead of one."

I swing my attention to Javen, whose face has fallen. Though his eyes glint with anger.

"We won't be able to bring everyone across on Earth, of course. First, we'll take a sample population over to build, like we've done here in Primaro. Then once a new city is complete, those deemed appropriate—the best minds, the young, the strong, as well as those who can afford to pay—can cross over. And Earth will have a new start."

My heart drops. So, who doesn't get to go? What'll happen to everyone not chosen?

"The people on Earth will riot," Luca says quietly. "They won't accept that only a selected percentage will have a chance to cross over."

Hammond taps her fingernails on her desk as if annoyed that Luca hadn't heard a word she had said. After a few seconds, she leans back into her chair and says, "As I shared earlier, *our hope* is that the Starfire's power will rejuvenate the damage on Earth. We'll use this to create *their hope*. And there's a chance the plan might work, but we can't risk losing everything when the chance at a new world is within our grasp."

"Will the ore mining affect the Intersection on Arcadia?" Luca asks.

Hammond redirects her attention to her screen for a few moments and then peers up at Luca. "With the mass removal of ore, we believe it will collapse the other side."

Javen gasps.

"Killing all the Alku?" Luca's mouth falls open, and then he clamps it and wipes any trace of horror from his expression.

"We've estimated their populations to *only* be a few hundred thousand. It's a sacrifice those on the World Senate are willing to make. We can't bring the Alku to this side permanently because of the tensions that their presence will create. It's just not possible. We tried to negotiate with their leaders, and they would not cooperate."

I catch Javen's attention, and he shakes his head no.

My stomach clenches at Hammond's lies.

"We've modified Richard Foster's terraforming program focus from harvesting to a project called Renewal. Tomorrow those simulations will begin, and mining the day after. You will meet Cassiopeia Foster first thing in the morning to have her commence work on this project. But she's to know nothing about her father's discovery or the Alku."

Luca stares at his hands, clasped tight in his lap. "Cassi ran out on me tonight at our dinner. I don't think she trusts me," he admits, eventually looking back up.

Hammond arches her eyebrow once more. "You're smart, right? Figure out a way to remedy the problem."

CHAPTER 17

When Luca leaves Hammond's office, we slip out behind him and use the stairs. We beat Luca to the exit, and as he opens the front with his ID, we race out the door and onto the street.

Breathless, I grab for Javen's arm and stop him.

"Your people are going to die if we don't figure out a way to end the mining. Do they understand this is what Hammond is planning?"

"Most have not been willing to fight. So . . . I don't believe they do."

I touch his arm. "You must tell them. There's no other choice at this point. I'll go with you. I recorded the whole conversation." I tap my Connect, realizing the video function is still active.

A measure of panic enters his eyes. "No, you can't come. The Council might accept you, but my uncle Wirrin and his supporters will not. For now, he's bound to the Council, but bringing you to my side of the Intersection may be too much for those in disagreement with the Council."

"Do you think you can convince them on your own?"

"There must be a middle ground, and I'll try to find it."

The air charges between us as the situation's gravity and the intensity between us swells. I wrap my arms around Javen's neck, savoring the feel of him once more. The air leaves his chest, with sorrow or with longing, I can't tell. Perhaps both. Standing on my toes, I lift my face, my mouth seeking his. And then, with desperation, my lips dance across his to the melody of my thrumming pulse as a mountain of emotions threatens to consume me. Reluctantly I ease away a few seconds later, whispering, "Please, Javen, come back to me."

"I'll always come back to you, Cassiopeia," he whispers in reply, a bit breathless. Looking around, Javen pulls me to a secluded spot in the shadow of a building. "The Starfire will release you now, so you must be careful."

I nod, my tongue unable to form words, and then he vanishes in front of me. Taking a second to gather my bearings, I inhale deeply. I check my Connect and a message alert from Irene appears on the screen.

There's something you'll want to see. Come as soon as you can.

I message Max and tell him to come to the dorm. Whether Irene hacked into the feed or was able to access the thumb drive, Max should be there too. Max's message buzzes almost immediately in reply.

I'm on my way.

I race for the dorm, avoiding people on the street. A woman looks my way as I brush past her. I had almost forgotten that people can see me now.

"Sorry," I say without stopping.

At the dorm, Max is already there and about to enter the building's front door.

"Max," I call out, and he turns my way.

"Was Irene able to access the drive?" he asks.

"I'm not sure. I haven't been home all night."

"Well, let's find out together." Max smiles and the expression makes me feel guilty for tonight with Javen. I want to tell Max everything. He's like my best friend here.

We fly out of the elevator and I say to Irene, "What did you find?" as I open the door to my room.

Irene looks up from a chair in the living area. Her jaw is tense. "Oh, Max. You're here too?"

"Cassi messaged me to come."

Irene glances at me, a worried glimmer in her eyes. "Well, shut the door."

"It's okay he's here, right?" I ask.

"You're going to need to be the judge of that," she says. "But if he doesn't mind getting wrapped up in information that could probably get us all arrested, then be my guest."

Max looks at me, his lips forming a straight line for a moment. "I'm already involved. I'm not going to back out now."

"Then I want him to stay." I grab a computer chair and pull it alongside Irene as Max does the same.

"I still haven't been able to get my hands on the equipment necessary to access the thumb drive," Irene says, pairing her DataPort to the media screen. "The hardware wasn't available at work. But I have a friend who does hacking on the side too, and she thinks she can get it tomorrow."

An image flashes onto the screen and my breath catches. I knew Irene would be showing us the ship's bay on the day of the explosion. But I didn't quite know how seeing the footage would affect me. Sickness swirls in my stomach as the feed starts. Staff mill around in the space while preparing the passengers who will disembark.

Max must notice my anxiety and leans forward to set his hand on top of mine. "You can do this," he whispers.

I grab his hand and squeeze, then let go. "Thank you for being here."

His lips quirk into a sad smile.

"This is too early," Irene mutters and swipes her fingers across the screen to move the feed to the correct time frame. "Okay, this should be right."

I watch as the staff sets up the buffet near where I first saw Javen. He's not there, but I have no clue if I'd be able to see him on a video anyway, or if he was even in the bay at that time.

"There." Irene points to the screen's left.

My stomach tightens as Luca comes into the frame. The security video's quality isn't great, but it's obvious the guy on the screen is Luca. He walks over to the stage area where Hammond had made her speech and then pivots to the left, closer to the location of the first explosion. He looks around and opens his coat but then turns his back, blocking my ability to see what he's doing.

"Can you zoom in?" My heart pounds.

Irene shrugs. "I can, but it's not going to give you much more information. With all the technology on the ship, you'd think the security system would be better." She pauses the video and uses her fingers on the screen to both rewind and enlarge.

I lean forward as the three of us watch the scene again.

"What is Luca doing?" Max asks.

Irene pauses the feed again. "Could he have planted the bomb?"

My breathing speeds up, and I lean to the back of my chair, considering the possibilities. "I don't get it," I finally say. "What good would it do for Luca, or anyone from the Board, to plant a bomb? If they were trying to kill my dad, it's a sloppy way to do it. They'd have no idea if he'd be one of the casualties. I'm no fan of Luca or Hammond, but this doesn't feel right."

"There's more you should see," Irene says.

She fast-forwards, and on the right side of the screen, Dad appears. He stands as if he's waiting, and then he turns and Luca joins him. With the low quality and no sound, it's difficult to tell what's going on. Their body language, however, suggests an argument. Dad backs away from Luca and raises a pointed finger at him. Luca spins from the conversation and walks off, head held high and shoulders stiffened. Just as he leaves, another man, who if I remember right may be on Dad's science team, hands him something. The man is bald and stocky. Dad takes the item, pockets it and rubs his hands over the tops of his arms as if he's cold. The man parts ways from Dad and walks to the same area Luca was a moment earlier.

And then I see him. Javen . . . no, not Javen. I squint at the screen. The person looks a lot like Javen, but it's not him . . . he's older. He grabs my dad from behind, and they both vanish. A split second later the explosion sends people and pieces of the interior flying.

I gasp and whip my attention to Max and Irene. "Did you see that?"

"Okay. You saw the same thing. I thought I was crazy. But Dr. Foster walked away from the man who handed him something and then disappeared," Irene says.

Max is wide-eyed.

"Wait," I say. "Didn't you see the other man too? The one who grabbed Dad right before the explosion?"

Irene squints at me in confusion. "There was no one else." Her gaze moves from my face down to my neckline.

"What's that?" Max says to me.

I look down to the Starfire, which is glowing beneath my dress. I slam my hand over the crystal to block the glow. "There was another man," I mutter, hoping the distraction works.

While still holding the DataPort, Irene throws her free hand onto her hip. "I already thought this whole thing was weird. And now it's getting weirder. So, start talking."

I stare at both of my friends. "You're never going to believe me."

"We both just saw your father disappear into thin air, Cassi," Max says. "That in itself seems unbelievable."

"It's not likely the feed has been tampered with," Irene says. "And even if it were, why would someone make the footage look like Dr. Foster disappeared?"

Nervousness races around in my chest, but then a thought hits me. "If this is real, my dad is alive. He didn't die in the explosion."

"But where is he?" Max asks.

The excitement rushes from me. "With the Alku."

"The Alku?" Irene asks as she sets the DataPort down.

I reach under my collar to pull out the Starfire, which has stopped glowing. I unhook the clasp and hold the crystal out. "This is a piece of the ore Hammond talked about on the announcement."

"How did *you* get it?" Irene asks.

"I was holding my dad's jacket when the explosion happened. The crystal was inside a pocket."

My thoughts flit across several options on how to explain the Starfire and Javen's people. But every single one sounds ridiculous. Then a thought comes to me. I have no idea if it will work, but I was able to call on the Starfire's power to cross me over to Javen's side of the Intersection. So I might be able to use it to make them understand.

"Can you rewind to the part before my dad vanishes? Right after he argues with Luca?"

Irene raises her eyebrow as if she thinks I'm stalling.

"Please," I ask.

She picks up the computer again and swipes to the earlier time frame. The feed starts.

"Now, I need you both to touch the crystal in my hand." I open my palm and reveal the Starfire. They both give me a look of confusion but do as I ask. I gesture with my head to the large screen. "Now watch."

Max and Irene turn their attention to the screen, and my stomach turns as I once again watch my dad walk away from the argument. From nowhere, the man who reminds me of Javen appears.

"Where'd that guy—?" Irene asks.

But before she gets the words out, Dad and the man disappear.

Irene removes her hand from me and pauses the feed.

"Did you see him too?" I ask Max.

"Uh . . . that man wasn't there the first time we watched," he says.

"Yes, he was. You just couldn't see him. He cloaked himself from our view."

Irene plops on the floor. "Well, who was he?"

I take a deep breath. "He's an Alku. They live on Arcadia. They were here before us."

Irene's mouth goes slack and Max leans in, his hands clasped as I explain everything. I tell them about the Alku, the Starfire, the Intersection, but I hold back on the conversation I heard between Hammond and Luca. They can know about the Starfire and how mining it will affect the Alku. But until I find out more, I don't want to share how the Earth will die in five years.

Then I tell them about Javen rescuing me in the bay and how we have this connection I don't understand. Max gently pulls away from me and stares at his hands. My heart sinks to my stomach. Before I can say anything to Max, Irene speaks again.

"You think the disappearing-guy was one of these Alku?" she asks.

Max remains silent, brows knitted together.

"That's the only explanation. It's the reason you could see him with the help of the Starfire."

"So, basically, Hammond is planning to mine all the Starfire and send the ore to Earth?" Max finally asks. "Even though she knows doing so could collapse the Alku side of the Intersection?"

I nod, relieved he's still engaged. "They could all die," I choke out, "and she's not allowing them to cross over to this side."

"Then we need to help them," Max says with a sad smile my way. "I want to heal the Earth too. But it's wrong to take from the Alku to do it. There must be a better way."

Irene lifts a grim smile as well. "I'm in too. What do we need to do next?"

CHAPTER 18

I shoot off my pillow as rustling sounds drift up from below. I peer over the side of my bunk and see Irene packing up her bag for work.

"I was about to wake you. I wasn't sure if you'd set an alarm."

I rub my eyes. "Letting Max stay here until 3:00 a.m. was a bad idea."

"Especially when you need to be sharp for your first day on the job." She lifts an eyebrow. "Okay . . . so my friend is meeting me before work to give me the equipment needed to access the data on your dad's drive. As soon as I find something, I'll let you know."

I throw my legs over the side of the bed and reach for the ladder to climb down. "Sounds good," I say as my feet hit the floor. "Hopefully, there's data we can use on it."

Irene throws her bag over her shoulder. "So, how do you get in contact with this guy Javen to find out if he told his people about Hammond's plan?"

"That's the thing. I don't really understand how the Starfire works. I tried calling for him last night, but nothing happened. I'll just need to wait for him to come to me." My stomach churns. I need to know who that man was, the one who looked like Javen.

She sighs. "Well, for now, we need to gather as much information as possible."

"Hopefully I can go through my dad's terraforming simulations today."

Irene opens her arms to me and pulls me into a hug. "We can do this. We're going to figure out where your dad is and stop Hammond from destroying the Alku."

I nod, trying to stay strong, but in truth, I wonder how in the world we're going to pull this off. She releases me and then exits the room.

I check the time and realize there's not enough for a shower. So instead, I pull on a pair of black pants and an aqua shirt from my drawer and fashion my hair into a low ponytail. I slip on a pair of comfortable boots for walking.

My Connect buzzes with a message from Max.

Don't be late. I'll see you there.

I'm leaving in a few minutes.

On the way out the door, I grab my bag from beside my bed and a peach from the fruit bowl, which I finish on my walk to the Capitol building. Once there, I pause on the street, gaze up at the building and say under my breath, "You can do this, Cassi."

I enter through the glass door at the front and check in at the ID station. Then, with a group of employees, I ride the elevator to the twentieth floor, the same location as Hirata's office. The door to the elevator opens, and I'm met by Luca, standing about ten feet away.

He turns to me and smiles. The expression sends a shiver down my spine since I still don't know if he was involved with the explosion on the ship or not. But I force a smile of my own.

"I saw you checked in at the ID station below, so I decided to meet you." Luca walks toward me as I step from the elevator's cab.

You mean Hammond told you to meet me here.

"I'm sorry you weren't feeling well last night. Did you go home?" He gestures me forward, down a hall to the right.

I grit my teeth. "Yes. I think with my job starting today, I was too nervous for any social interaction."

"I apologize if I made you feel uncomfortable in any way."

I nod, but his apology doesn't make me feel any better about him.

"Here's your office." Luca stops and opens a door marked "2015" to reveal a small room boasting a view of the city, complete with a desk and a touchscreen computer. "All the programs your father used are loaded for you to begin," he says as we step inside.

"And his older simulations? I'll need the files to study what worked and what didn't."

"If necessary for the project, those should be loaded as well." Luca stuffs his hands in his pockets and looks at the floor. "All your instructions for the current project should be on there too."

"Will Hammond be stopping by?"

He shakes his head. "Probably not today. She's out on location."

My eyes flit to him. "Location?"

"The mining site."

My stomach drops at his words, but there's nothing I can say at this point. "Well, maybe tomorrow."

"Yes." Luca presses his lips together and then lets out a sigh. "If you need me, send a message through the company system. I'll get it right away." With that he departs, sparing me a quick glance over his shoulder as he disappears through the door.

As I round the back of my desk, I look out over Primaro. The city is beautiful and, in my opinion, expertly integrated with the landscape of Arcadia. It's what Dad wanted. He'd hoped to build a new civilization that would be in harmony with the planet. Earth had destroyed itself, and he didn't want to repeat history. Unlike Hammond, who is planning to destroy the planet in a whole new way.

I bring my attention to the room I'm in and sit in the chair behind my desk. With a tap, I activate the screen and launch the terraforming program. It's the same one I've been training on for the last couple of years.

I open the current project, and a 3-D map of Arcadia's topography for the area around Primaro opens. On the left side of the map, about one hundred miles from the city boundary line, is an area marked "Mining Location #1." My eyes flit around, hunting, searching. Is there only one location? Zooming out, I purse my lips together in concentration—only one site that I can see.

I hide the window and access the older files, including Dad's simulations. I want to see his failed scenarios and at what point he moved the city farther away from the Starfire fields, like Javen said he had.

But as I scroll back, there are no sims from before the time he must have visited Arcadia with Mom. I slam my fist on the desk in a burst of frustration. Hammond isn't a fool. Why would she want me to have that information? If I did, I might start digging and find out too much.

A rap echoes on my door and I jump. "Um, come in?"

The door opens, and Max's face pops through the opening. "I see you made it."

"Yeah, I'm having a *great* time," I say while rolling my eyes.

"Well, hopefully, I can improve your mood. Hirata and Cooper are in a meeting and have a few things to discuss with you."

"What about Luca? He was just here."

Max shakes his head. "Luca is in Hammond's office downstairs. Come on."

I tap off the screen and rise, and Max escorts me to Hirata's office again.

"I'm not staying. But I'll wait outside," Max says.

"Okay," I say as he opens the door. Lia Hirata and Lawrence Cooper wait inside, studying a hologram of the planet. Cooper looks up at me and stands. A tense smile crosses his dark lips and he reaches out a hand, gesturing to a seat beside him.

It's been a while since I've seen Lawrence Cooper. But he worked with my dad, so we've crossed paths before. His short black hair has more light specks of gray mixed in it than I recall from a few months ago.

"Hello, Cassiopeia," Cooper says as Max closes the door behind me.

I politely smile at him and sit when he does. "You have questions?" I figure we might as well skip to the important stuff.

"We have an update on your father," Hirata says as she taps off the hologram.

"I didn't feel right to keep information from you anymore," Cooper says. "Richard is a good man, and I know what you are going through would cause him great pain."

"So . . ." I whip my attention between the two of them. "So, he's alive?"

Hirata sighs. "That's not what I said."

"Then what are you saying?" I ask.

"We are working to find out more," Cooper says. "But it's difficult."

I narrow my eyes. "You mean you think I'm too young to understand."

"Cassi," Hirata says and leans her elbows on the desk. "Please trust we are doing everything we can."

"Richard was my friend," Cooper says. "I want to do whatever I can to help his family."

I stare at them in silence. "This is about the Alku, isn't it?" If they deny my question then I won't push.

Nearly in unison, both Hirata and Cooper lean back into their seats and look at each other. If the situation weren't so dangerous, the scene would almost be comical. They definitely know.

"I'm aware of them," I say.

"How?" Cooper is the first to speak. "I know it wasn't Richard. He was sworn to secrecy."

"It doesn't matter how. But Max does too. And we both know about the Starfire and Earth." Tears sting at the corners of my eyes while the weight of the information bears down on me. "And that my dad's disappearance involves the Alku. I think the Alku saved him from the explosion—or at least tried to."

"You may be right, and we are trying to get more information. We didn't want to give you false hope," Cooper says.

"But you're not doing anything about the Starfire?"

Hirata sighs. "You *are* so young. You have no idea what it's like to go up against Hammond and the World Senate. If we push too far too fast, they'll simply find a way to remove us from the Board. Then there will be no one with differing views."

"Do you think the Senate was attempting to *remove* my father from the Board?" My mind shifts to the security feed and how Luca may have planted something in the bay.

"We don't have the answer to that question yet," Hirata says. "There's still a possibility the explosion was terrorist activity and Richard Foster simply got caught in the middle of it. Not everyone on Earth wanted us to settle Arcadia."

A chime resonates from Hirata's touchscreen.

"We need to wrap up the meeting." She looks to me. "I'll let you know as soon as any information I can share comes in. Promise."

Hirata stands, and Cooper follows her lead.

"Thanks for your time." I stand and turn for the door.

"I'm sorry we can't do more," Cooper says.

I lean toward him, lower my voice, and say, "There might come a time when you can. So, I'm going to hold you to your desire to do more." I don't wait for a response and exit the room.

Outside Max waits as he said he would, and I wave my hand for him to follow. Just as we start to walk, Alina rounds the corner, holding a package in her hands. A smile spreads over her lips when she sees us.

"Hey, you two," she says, her voice chipper. Way too chipper for my mood right now.

I paste on a smile. "Are you working here now?"

The three of us meet near the hall's opening. "Yes, I got the job I interviewed for." Alina glances at Max and gives him a grin.

"Good for you," Max says, his lips mashing together after he says it.

"It's not much, but it's a start. I was right. I'm basically a deliverer of coffee. But I know I'll get promoted when they see how dedicated I am. I just need to figure out a way to prove it."

In the office foyer, the elevator chimes and the doors slide away. Luca steps out.

Max touches my arm. "You should return to work, Cassi. I have to go too."

Alina turns in the direction we're looking and then to us. She squints in thought and then in confusion.

"I'll see you both later," Max says and walks back toward Hirata's office.

"Bye," I say and then swing my attention to Luca, whose back is to us. He's speaking to a person I don't know. Here's my chance to go to my office without him seeing me.

"Good luck with your job," I say to Alina and walk in the direction of my office. But she sticks to my side, apparently not taking the hint.

She leans into my ear and whispers, "Why are you trying to get away from Luca Powell?"

"Um, I'm not," I lie. "I need to work."

Alina continues to follow me to my door. I open it and look to her. "I'll see you later."

She lifts her hand to wave and realizes she still has a package in her hand. "Oh . . . this is for you. It's a rush delivery. Just came in."

"For me?"

"Yeah . . . apparently I deliver packages *and* coffee." She hands the parcel to me.

"Thanks."

"No problem." Alina turns and finally leaves.

I enter my office, shut the door, and then glance down at the box. There's no sender listed on the label, only where the package was sent from.

Extra Solar.

It must be Irene's.

CHAPTER 19

I touch the Starfire around my neck. "Where are you, Javen?" I mutter as I hold the thumb drive and a small, portable data viewer that Irene had sent over. I re-read the note tucked inside.

This might be the info we need. Check it out.

A part of me is dying to see the data, but the other part is terrified. It may not be what we need. And if the evidence is there, what if the Board won't listen?

I need air, so I throw the data viewer into my bag and exit my office. Outside, Luca is gone and there's no sign of Alina. Without anyone noticing me, I make it downstairs and swing around to the rear of the building to a bench. I inhale deeply as I check to make sure no one is around before I gather the data viewer from Irene in my bag. I plug in the thumb drive, and the files appear on the screen.

They're mostly videos.

I take another deep breath and tap the first one, marked around the date my parents were supposedly in Europe. My breath catches as I see Mom and Dad. Mom is smiling, and Dad wraps his arm around her waist and just stares at her.

She laughs and smacks him on the arm. "Make the video, Rich."

"I'm too busy looking at you," he says.

My eyes sting as tears form and my lips tremble while I touch her cheek on the screen. "Hi, Mom," I whisper, my voice shaky.

Mom chuckles and points to the camera. "The video."

"Fine." Dad steps aside to reveal an amazing scene. A vast hillside covered in a light cyan mist.

"These are the Starfire fields of Arcadia. We're not entirely sure what they do yet, but we are working on it. It's the reason we came here."

So, my parents *did* come to Arcadia.

The mist above the ground sparkles as it pirouettes and bends in the air. I touch the screen. My parents are so close to me.

The video stops and I choose one farther down the list.

This time Dad's in his office. The one in our home on Earth. He sighs and runs a hand through his hair, then looks at the camera.

"Hammond and the World Senate won't listen anymore. They're just avoiding any facts about how the Alku exist on Arcadia . . . or Paxon, as the Alku call their side of the Intersection. I guess when you discover people are occupying the same space on a different plane of existence, it's easy to write it all off as impossible. After one visit, Hammond won't even cross the Intersection to meet with their Council. On the other hand, Isabel and I have practiced with the Starfire crystals given to us by Vihann, the leader of the Alku. It has allowed us to bridge a mind connection to him while also allowing us to communicate in a way I didn't understand at first. It's as if we are in a dream that spans the universe."

Memories of my dreams of Javen, after he rescued me from the bay, bubble to the surface. Was this the kind of experience Dad was talking about?

"These are incredible people who've lived their lives so differently than the people on Earth. They have everything they need through the Starfire and live in complete harmony with their world. There's so little discord among the people. But our coming to Arcadia might threaten this. So, I've started work on a plan that I'm calling 'Renewal.' The first step was convincing the

Board to move the city away from the field, and with coaxing, they've allowed me. And after I explained how the Earth is in such terrible shape, the Alku Council helped form a solution. We can mine the older Starfire crystals; the Alku call them seeds. Their Council already agrees those may be harvested and taken to Earth. These can essentially be planted to start a renewal of the planet. It'll take time and a lot of hard work, but the Earth will eventually improve. Our people *can* live in symbiosis." Dad leans into his seat and rubs his face. "But the World Senate is too impatient. There's talk that the Earth's time is short, but I'll know whether we can begin Renewal once the repopulation ships arrive. But I'm afraid the temptation to make money off the crystals is too strong. At this point, the Alku don't have a means to protect the fields. I must make the Board listen." His lips form a tight line, his eyes sadden, and then the video goes black.

Attached to the video is a map of future cities, with areas blocked off for just the Alku and separate areas for Earth colonization. He outlines ways new buildings can be erected to not harm the Starfire fields on our side of the Intersection.

So, Javen's people have already made a compromise that will help Earth. And Dad said his plan would work. Why isn't the Board doing this? Why aren't Hirata and

Cooper fighting harder for a solution where everyone can win?

I tap the last video on the list, and my stomach turns when I see the date. It's around noon on the day of the Gala. The same day Hammond caught Dad in the meeting I overheard.

On the screen, Dad slams his fist onto his desk. "We got all the way here, and Hirata and Cooper aren't going to support me! Hammond storms into one meeting and now they're too scared to go up against her." He looks straight into the camera. "Well, I'm not. Coming here was my and Isabel's dream. I won't have that dream tainted by greed and cowardice. I'm going to the Gala tonight, and I will show everyone the beauty of Arcadia. Then, when I get to the surface, I'll meet with the Alku Council again. I think I have a way to protect the fields with or without the Board."

I grit my teeth, and my hands form fists. Hammond and the World Senate cannot be allowed to steal from and murder Javen's people! The Alku offered help and allowed us to settle on their planet without resistance.

Earth must know. I won't allow this darkness to continue. There must be a way to get the word out. I pocket the thumb drive and stuff the data viewer into my bag and then message Irene and Max.

Meet me as soon as you can after work.

At this point, I don't have any option but to go to my office and work on the mining project until the end of the day. If I leave work for too long, it might bring suspicion, and I can't have that. I race around the front of the building and into the entrance, dreading the next seven hours before I can get to my dorm and figure this all out.

Max is still stuck at work and Irene hasn't messaged me since this morning, but I check the time and know that she should be home soon.

I've watched Dad's videos two more times since I got back to the dorm, but I need for Irene and Max to see the footage before we come up with a way to speak to the more flexible members of the Board.

Maybe they didn't know there were alternatives for living with the Alku and healing Earth. If they can see the videos, too, I know their eyes will be opened. At this point, I can't see any other option. There's no way three kids are going to be able to change the minds of

Hammond, Luca, and the World Senate. We need pull from the other Board members and their connections.

Nervousness spins in my chest, and I close my eyes to call out to Javen again through the Starfire. But once more, nothing changes. It worked at the restaurant; why isn't it working now?

Even though I have no desire to eat, I decide that I might be able to force down a sandwich. A knock sounds at the door before I reach the kitchen, however, and I swing around. Max!

I rip open the door.

"Hey," says Alina. She pokes her head in through the door. "Where's Irene?"

In surprise, I withdraw, unfortunately giving Alina additional space to come in.

"Uh, she's still at work I guess."

Alina slips past me. "How was your first day on the job?"

I close the door and try to think of a way to get rid of her, but nothing comes to mind.

She drops into the nearest chair and my attention trains on the data viewer on the side table. My first instinct is to grab it. Alina is so nosy there's not much stopping her from noticing the tech and wanting to take a peek.

"It was . . . long," I finally answer, diverting my attention to her.

"Same for me." She glances around and locks on to the viewer. "What's this? Looks old."

My heart jumps, and I lean forward to snag the drive from her hands. "Um. It's . . . vacation videos my dad made."

Alina pinches her lips together. "I'm really sorry he died."

I drop the data viewer to my side and sigh. "See, that's the thing. I don't think he did." I know I shouldn't breathe a word of this, but the more people who can see how Hammond isn't completely trustworthy, the better. "President Hammond might be covering up the explosion."

Alina narrows her eyes in confusion. "What?"

"I have information."

"Like what?"

I shake my head. "I can't tell you. But I can say Hammond is keeping a lot of information from the people."

"Why would she do that?" Alina asks.

"Because there are things about Arcadia she doesn't want everyone to know."

Alina opens her mouth to speak, but my Connect buzzes and I don't hear what comes out of her mouth as I look at the words on the clear screen.

Get out of your dorm now. Irene was taken into custody. I'm on my way.

"Uh . . . I gotta go." I race for the door and reach for the handle.

"What's going on?" Alina asks.

I round to her. "If anyone comes for me, tell them I left and you don't know where I went. And forget everything I just told you about my dad. I didn't mean to get you all wrapped up in this mess."

I throw open the door and race down the hall.

CHAPTER 20

I race out of the building, and a vehicle screeches to a halt right behind me. I glimpse over my shoulder and my heart nearly leaps out of my chest as the door flies open and a figure jumps out.

I don't wait to see who the person is and take off down the sidewalk.

"Cassi!" a male voice shouts from behind.

I swing around to the voice. Max is sprinting toward me.

I skid to a stop as he catches up to me and grabs my arm. "Hirata sent me to bring you to her. She can protect you."

"Hirata and Cooper have been almost useless in this whole mess."

"They're doing what they can."

I yank my arm from his hand. "Well, it's not enough. So, what makes you think they're going to be able to keep Hammond from locking me away or worse?"

Our Connects buzz at the same time, and I glance down. The hologram activates, and my eyes widen at the words scrolling across it—something about a group of people who are not committed to the new direction of Arcadia's settlement and, therefore, must be located and detained.

Irene's face flashes onto the screen as already found. Several other unfamiliar faces appear and then a girl with long strawberry blond hair—me!

I swing my head around, looking for other people who might recognize my face, but the street in front of my dorm is pretty sparse. And I'm not waiting around to see if any people within the vicinity notice me.

"I . . . I have to go." I turn and dart down the sidewalk again. But Max keeps to my side.

"Where are you going to go, Cassi? The authorities are going to find you."

"The only place I know the Board can't follow for now."

"And where's that? Your best chance is for me to take you to Hirata. She promised to help," he pants as he runs alongside me.

I don't answer him and keep running full speed, focusing on the Starfire around my neck.

I have to get to Javen, to his people, to his side of the Intersection.

As I run, the space around me shifts and bends, making my stomach roil. But I press on, concentrating. This has to work.

A cyan glow surrounds me and a crack in space appears. I jump for the break as a hand grabs my arm again from behind. I plunge to the ground with a thump. A person crashes on top of me, and I let out a groan. Pain rakes up my side, and I push Max off of me.

Max scrambles to his feet and looks around, eyes wide. "What the . . . where are we?"

I swing my attention up. The city buildings are gone. Max and I ended up in an open field, flanked by forest. Above us, a cyan mist hovers in the darkening sky.

"On the other side." I breathe a sigh of relief and stand as I wipe the dust from my clothes.

"The other side? The other side of *what*?" His brows crease in confusion. "I was running to catch you. All I did was grab your arm, and then we are here, out in the middle of nowhere."

"We're on the other side of the Intersection." My stomach drops. "Did you see the entrance?"

"I didn't see anything. We were there and then suddenly here."

My nervousness dissipates. "We need to find the Alku and get help."

Max lifts his hands and takes a step back. "Okay, we've gone through this before, but this is crazy."

"I know, but it's real. Hammond can't just take the Alku's world away from them."

Max looks around. "Fine, I'm just going to ignore that whatever is happening is completely nuts. But where are these people? Are you sure they're even here?"

I exhale a long breath as I realize I don't know the answer to that question. I have only seen Javen and two others. They could be right over the hill or a thousand miles away. Panic starts to rise in me. What if we *are* out in the middle of nowhere? I have no idea where to go if Javen doesn't find us. And is he even aware we're here?

With a deep breath, I push away the thoughts. I brought Max and myself across a whole dimension; I'm not going to get us lost in the woods.

"I have an idea." I sit on the ground and close my eyes.

"What are you doing?" Max asks.

"Give me sec. I just need a little quiet." I keep my eyelids shut. "I'm new to this whole thing."

"Okay."

In my mind I let all my thoughts settle, and I focus on Javen. I focus on his face and bronzed skin. I focus on his voice and how the sound fills me with music. I focus on how his arms feel encircling my body.

Like a magnet, I pull his presence closer, and like a mist his consciousness surrounds me. I open my eyes, and Javen sits before me, a crooked smile on his lips. He leans forward and presses his mouth to mine, and as he does, my body longs for him. I run my hands over his shoulders.

But remembering Max, I snap back and flit my attention to him.

Max still stands to my side, his mouth agape, and what might be hurt fills his expression.

"Um," I say, feeling embarrassment and guilt all wadded up in my stomach. "This is Javen."

Javen spins to Max in surprise. He must not have known another person was here. "You brought someone with you?"

"That's Max. He came by accident."

Javen stands and is nearly a head taller than Max. The two stare, sizing each other up.

"We need your help, Javen," I finally say. "Hammond knows I've been digging up information about my dad and she sent out an alert for my detainment. My face has been shown to every member of the city. And my roommate was already taken into custody."

Javen looks at me. "Why was she taken?"

"Because Irene knows too much. And Max does too, but Hammond is apparently not aware of that yet."

Max loosens his tense shoulders and squares himself. "I'm working for one of the Board members who is open to opposing Hammond. But she needs support. Without it, she can make very few moves. If your people can help, there may be others who will rise up."

Javen gaze slides back to me. "I've told you, most of my people are resistant to fighting."

"But not all," I say. "Your uncle is willing to resist."

"The Council still wants to settle on a peaceful resolution to this situation. War will change our people, our way of life. It's not who we are anymore."

"But your people might die. Please let us talk to them."

"Us?" Javen asks and looks at Max and me. "I can't take you both to the Council. They'll never accept it."

"Then just take me," I say.

Javen presses his lips together and finally says, "You do have an unusual connection to the Starfire. Maybe my people will see that and know your heart is true."

I look to Max. "We need to send you to the other side. Hammond isn't searching for you, so go and try to find out more about Irene's location. Maybe Hirata can have her released or at least ensure her safety."

Max nods and I can't tell what he's really thinking or feeling. "You message me as soon as you get back, okay?" A worried smile softens his expression.

I smile at him in return. "I will," I say, hoping he sees that I do care about him.

Javen touches Max on the shoulder, and they both vanish. But in a split second, Javen returns. He catches my gaze and then pulls me into his arms.

"You summoned me," Javen says into my ear.

"Summoned?"

"The method my people use to call each other through the Starfire."

"Maybe it works that way for everyone. You just haven't tested it," I say.

"I could be wrong," Javen says, "but I don't think so. Your father could not make summoning work, no matter how hard he tried."

I squint in thought. "You did say the Starfire linked us. Maybe our connection is allowing me to use the crystal's power."

Javen sighs. "Yes, but I've never seen anything like it. All I can hope is that my people will see this bond as a good thing."

I lay my head on Javen's chest and drink him in. "Take me to them."

CHAPTER 21

"I'm bringing them to you," Javen takes my hand. "When a gathering is necessary, we summon our people through the Starfire."

"All of them?"

"No, not all, mostly representatives as well as the Council. But the Starfire will"—he stops as if he's searching for the word—"will transmit to all of my people so they're aware of whatever is decided."

My chest clenches at the thought of all of Javen's people watching me.

"I'll make sure you have the chance to speak," he says. "I can make no guarantees it'll change their minds, though."

I nod. "I'm ready."

Javen squeezes my hand and closes his eyes.

I study how his body relaxes and how the space around us grows still in response. Below my chin, the

Starfire I wear begins to pulse and glow, and a familiar chill encompasses my body. A thought hits me. I was bundling up on the ship, same as Dad, unlike everyone else. Was it my connection to the planet?

My body shudders and a cyan glow emits around Javen and me. A jumble of voices permeates my mind. The sound grows louder and more chaotic—some angry, some curious and some excited. I let go of Javen's hand and drop to my knees, covering my ears, but it's no use since the voices are not coming from the outside. I grit my teeth against the sound and look up at Javen, who's still in a trance.

My Starfire pulses faster and the glow around us presses into my body with such force that I struggle to draw breath. I open my mouth to tell Javen to stop just as the feeling releases, and I fall to the ground in a heap.

"Cassi!" Javen says and drops next to me. "Are you okay?"

I gasp and all the compression on my body and mind is gone. "I . . . I think so."

"My people don't usually learn to use the Starfire so quickly. The power must be overwhelming you." His face fills with concern.

I straighten. "I'm fine."

Javen stands and holds out his hand. I take it, and he pulls me up.

"Where are they?" I scan the landscape. "Your people."

"They'll be here."

"But you came so quickly when I summoned you. I opened my eyes, and you were there."

Javen smiles. "That's because I always want to be at your side. My people will require more convincing."

Warmth from his words fills me, making me almost forget about the pain I endured while he summoned his people.

I begin to relax when the space around us lights up as far as I can see. I raise my hand to shield against the glare. Silent figures begin to appear, and my breathing speeds up. *Here we go.*

Javen interlaces his fingers in mine, and the action instantly calms my nerves.

Like flashes of light, more people appear—some as singles, others in groups—until a large crowd completely encircles us. Beyond them, the grasses and trees sparkle with flickering lights, as if fed by their energy.

Javen squares himself and plants his feet as a man appears about ten feet in front of us. My breath hitches at the sight of the man.

He's tall with dark hair and his eyes swirl with cyan. He's the person who made my dad disappear as seen on the explosion's video feed. I flit my attention between Javen and the man. Javen releases my hand and steps forward, then bends on one knee. He bows his head for a beat and looks up.

"Thank you for coming, Father."

Father? This is Javen's father? My mind races and excitement bubbles in my chest. Then he might know if Dad is alive.

The man nods, and Javen stands. But then his father locks his stare onto me and my chest constricts.

"Who is this?" the man asks in a rich voice that sinks deep into my core and rattles my waning confidence.

Javen straightens his shoulders and raises his head high. "This is Cassiopeia Foster. She's from Earth and has requested to speak with the Council."

Javen's father doesn't drop his attention from me, but his gaze softens a fraction.

Three women and two men step ahead of the crowd and join Javen's father.

"Javen," says a woman with long white hair and pale skin, whose eyes also shift between cyan and brown. "You know it is against our custom to bring in an outsider without the consent of the Council."

Javen turns to her. "I know. But Cassiopeia is Richard Foster's daughter."

The woman, dressed in a long white tunic, tips her head in interest.

A man with dark salt and pepper hair and an angular face steps forward. I stare at him. "Nevertheless," he says, "the Council has the right to refuse anyone to come to our side of the Intersection. I will not have this intrusion." The man glares at me and the expression sends a shiver down my spine.

I scan the crowd of people. They remain silent as if they're merely taking in everything being said. Javen's people are as diverse as the passengers who came from Earth to Arcadia. Some are short, while others are tall, and their skin ranges dark to light. The only difference is the limited hair color, which seems to either be dark brown, nearly black, or white.

"The Starfire has chosen her," Javen announces.

A collective gasp from the people whips my attention around to Javen.

"What?" I ask.

Javen's father tilts his head. "That's not possible, Javen. Only our people are born of Starfire and can be chosen by it. Outsiders are not."

Holding his head high, Javen keeps his stare locked onto his father. "Cassiopeia has linked with the Starfire and crossed over the Intersection two times on her own. This gives her the right to be heard by the Council."

The three women and two men gather around Javen's father and speak in hushed tones.

I study the group of Alku Council members. Did Dad and Mom meet with them all when they were here? Were they friends with my parents, and if so, does that mean they will be friends with me? I have so many questions I can't ask. Nausea from waiting to hear what the Alku will say coils in my belly and I run my trembling hands over my midsection.

Finally, they part and Javen's father looks directly at me. "Please step toward the Council, Cassiopeia Foster."

I inhale deeply and put one foot in front of the other, trying my best to ignore my shaking legs and the many pairs of eyes staring my way.

"Yes, sir," I say to him when I stand about three feet away.

He holds out his hand to me. "My name is Vihann. I am the chosen leader of my people." He pauses. "May I please have your hand?"

I offer it to him, and the moment my fingers touch his, my mind goes blank.

With a snap, the world returns to me, and I gasp for breath.

Vihann holds my gaze and releases my hand. "You are bound to my son, as well," he whispers to me as he furrows his brows in confusion.

My breathing speeds up. Bound to Javen? I know we had discussed our connection, but that sounds official.

"My son is correct," Vihann says in a much louder voice. "This Earthling has been chosen by the Starfire, and this gives her the right to be heard."

Each of the Council members nods in agreement and Vihann stretches out his hand to gesture me to the people.

I turn and look to Javen, whose face is full of hope.

I wish I were so confident, but I gulp down my fear since I've never spoken in front of a crowd of this size. Convincing the Alku isn't going to be easy.

As best as I can, I tell the Council and the gathered people everything I know: that Hammond and the World Senate plan to mine and take the Starfire to Earth to create an Intersection to a new world; that there are members of the Board who are more reasonable and may help. I tell them that I know of an alternative that my father was working on, a project he called Renewal.

"Hammond knows you are unwilling to resist, so she's just going to take the Starfire from you," I say with all eyes on me.

When I'm done, Vihann frowns and addresses the Council. "We are aware of all of this. Scouts have been sent to your side and have seen your ships and mining equipment coming to the surface. We have nothing here to stop their plans from happening."

"Not true," a female voice shouts from the crowd.

I swing around to the source and watch as a young woman pushes her way through the people. My jaw tenses. It's Beda, Javen's cousin. She wears a pair of form-fitting cotton pants and a sleeveless tank. Scowling, she glares at me as she walks forward.

Why? I have no idea. I'm the one trying to help.

She steps between Vihann and me, looking his way now. "You know there *is* another way. It's been done before."

"Beda," Vihann says. "You are my kin, so I will allow this intrusion to pass."

"Uncle," she growls and picks up her booted foot and slams it to the ground. "There are those of us willing to risk it."

Beda still scares me, but she really is the voice of reason here. I look to Javen, but he only glances away.

Vihann puffs up. "Our ancestors were violent. Using the Starfire in the way you speak relives their mistakes. Our people will only use the Starfire for good."

My heart clenches as I hear his words.

"What if you could use the alternative my father spoke of? The older Starfire can be given to help heal Earth." I step to Beda's side, and her feet remain planted.

Vihann returns his attention to me. "Your father is gone."

My breath hitches at his mention of Dad. Vihann is aware of what happened to him. But I push the thoughts away. Now is not the time. "Then come to the other side. Show yourself to the people in Primaro. Hammond is hiding your existence, but if everyone knows you are here, then there'll be those who will stand up for you. No one will be able to deny that the Alku are real."

"If what you say about Hammond is true, it will start a war the Council is not willing to engage in," he says.

Beda bares her teeth at Vihann. "You are all cowards." She flings her hand at me. "Only this stinking Earthling is not." She twists and pushes her way back through the crowd.

"If the people of Earth simply knew of your existence, I'm certain there would be support to work out a solution to benefit everyone involved," I say. "Make yourselves visible. Bring your people to our side of the Intersection."

Vihann raises his head and studies me. "I'm very sorry, Cassiopeia Foster, but we will not cross over the Intersection to your side to prove our existence to your people."

"But it would be better than staying here and dying," I cry out.

Vihann tips his head. "I don't think you fully understand. Staying on your side of the Intersection is not a permanent solution for us. We can only renew ourselves with the Starfire on this side, and without the ability to renew, the Alku will die anyway."

CHAPTER 22

Javen and I are left standing in the field as the last of his people disappear.

"What did Vihann mean that your people will die on my side of the Intersection? You have been fine there."

"You saw what happened after we jumped from that window in the Capitol building."

"But you had been shot. That was different."

Javen's shoulders slump. "It was extreme, not different. We have used the Starfire for so long that it almost functions as a life-force of my people, almost like eating and drinking."

"And you can't do this on the other side?"

"It only works on this side."

"Then why won't your people listen?" I shout. "They are just lying down and giving up."

"Because my father is right. Our ancestors used the Starfire for evil. People were enslaved, and wars were great and terrible."

"And you think Hammond and the World Senate won't try to misuse the Starfire themselves? The cycle will only repeat itself."

Javen lets out a deep sigh.

"If the Alku will not save themselves, then I'm going to try," I say. "My dad wanted our people to live in peace, and I'm not going to let him down." I think for a moment and come up with a plan. There's probably no way it'll work, but I don't have time for Hirata and Cooper. "We need to go to the other side and locate Irene."

"Irene? Why? You said she had been detained."

"She has, but Max is working on finding out where she's being held and then convincing Hirata and Cooper to have her released. If you can get us into the Capitol building, Irene can help me do what I need to do."

"You can't do this, Cassi . . . you saw what happened to your father for trying to help us."

I gaze up at Javen. "My dad's not dead, and your father knows where he is."

Javen's eyes widen. "What are you talking about?"

"On the video Irene showed me, Vihann was there, and he disappeared with my Dad right before the explosion."

"I don't understand. Why wouldn't my father tell you?"

"I . . . I have no idea. But intuition tells me that he's alive, and we must show the settlers your people exist. I also think one of the Council members had something to do with the explosion."

Javen eases back in shock. "Who?"

"I'm not sure yet. But I recognized a man from the feed. He was in the same area the blast came from." I steel myself and hold out my hand to Javen.

He entwines his fingers with mine but looks away from me and out over the field, whispering, "My people wouldn't hurt others."

"Javen," I whisper back, "'if I don't try and find out the truth, you'll die and . . . and I may also never see my dad again." My chest tightens. "I've already lost so much. Please. I need you."

His eyes return to me and his jaw tightens when a tear slips down my cheek. I'm asking him to betray his father and his people. He doesn't say anything, but I sense his understanding. Relief touches my pulse until another fear enters my mind. If I'm caught, I have no idea what Hammond will do to me. Kill me? What will happen to Javen if his father learns of his involvement to help me? I push away all my fears and ignore the ache of never seeing Javen or my dad again.

"It's time," I say with more confidence than I feel.

I wipe away my tears and then close my eyes, visualizing the two of us on my side of the Intersection. Energy pulses through me, and when I open my eyes, Javen and I stand beyond the edge of the city under a cluster of trees.

My Connect buzzes, and I tap the face. A holographic message pops up from Max.

I was able to locate Irene. She's being held at the Detainment Center. Cell 408. That's all the information I could get.

"Show me the Detainment Center's location," I say into my Connect. The display shows our current location in relation to Irene's. It's at least two miles away. "Can we just . . . teleport there?"

Javen shakes his head. "It would take too much energy. We need to reserve the Starfire's strength in case of an emergency. But I can cloak us." He takes my hand. "Don't let go, or you'll become visible."

I grasp onto him, and we begin to run through the dark city streets.

On the way, my pulse drums in my ears as we pass the occasional security vehicle and pedestrian. As each passes by without seeing us, I let out a sigh of relief.

I look up as we finally make it to the Detainment Center.

"408," I say. "Can we grab Irene from inside and bring her out here?"

Javen thinks for a moment. "It will drain my energy to take you both."

"Then I'll hide while you get her. Then we need to get into the Capitol building."

We race into the shadows of the walkway between the Detainment Center and the neighboring building.

Javen squeezes my hand. "See you soon." He lets go of my hand and vanishes.

I press my back against the wall of the building, knowing I'm now fully visible. Panting from our run, I hang my head and bring my hand to the Starfire pendant. Nervousness crushes my chest.

"I know you're out there, Dad, and I'm going to find you," I whisper to the shadows.

The sound of pebbles crunching nearby jolts me back to reality and my eyelids shoot open. Right next to me is Javen with Irene in his arms, his hand covering her mouth as she struggles against him. Her wide eyes are the only part of her face I can see under the light of the moons and streetlights. If he lets her loose, she'll scream.

I peel off the wall and turn to them.

"It's okay, Irene, you're safe!" I whisper.

Her eyes relax when she sees me, and Javen loosens his grip. Irene wriggles from his grasp and thrusts her arms around my neck. "Cassi," she cries into my shoulder.

"We have you." I look to Javen. "But it's time to go."

"Cloaking all three of us is going to be difficult for me," Javen says.

I bring up directions to the Capitol building on my Connect. "It's not that far. All you have to do is get us there and into the building. Do you have enough reserves for that, you think?" He nods, though the movement is faint.

"What are we doing?" Irene says and turns around to Javen. "And who are you?"

"Javen," he says.

"Javen is one of the Alku. Hammond is starting the mining tomorrow, and we need to stop it. His people could die if we don't. I need your help. I'll explain when we get there."

Worry washes over Irene's face, but she nods. "I'm not sure I can be in any more trouble than I'm in anyway."

"Take Javen's hand and don't let go," I say.

Irene does as I say as I grab for Javen's other hand. Immediately, a colorful glow emits off our group. We race from the shadows and head toward the Capitol building. As we do, the blare of an alarm blasts behind us. The Detainment Center. They must have discovered Irene is missing.

Security vehicles speed by us and airships hover in the sky above, shining spotlights onto the street.

"Settlers of Primaro," a voice comes from one of the ships. "For your safety, please return to your homes immediately." The recording continues to play as we run, and my Connect buzzes with the same message.

"They're looking everywhere for us," I yell to Javen.

"Stay with me. I'll get you there."

But, just as he says it, I watch Irene stumble. She releases Javen's hand, and instantly the glow around her dissipates. Clinging to each other's hands, Javen and I skid to a stop. But the light of an airship snaps to her. Two vehicles on the ground stop and the doors fly open.

Irene raises her hands in surrender as officers exit their cars, weapons trained on her.

My heart stops in my chest and I almost cry out for my friend. Before I can, Javen swings his attention to me.

"Where do we need to go inside the Capitol building?"

The jumble of thoughts in my head works to coalesce. "Floor five," I somehow manage to say, then look to him, trying to tamp down the urge to panic. "But you'll use up all your energy."

"I have to get you both off the streets." With that, in what seems like slow motion, he pulls me toward Irene and holds his other hand out toward her.

When he makes contact, a cyan burst of light floods my vision, and when the color stops, I'm thrown into a wall. I inhale a sharp breath as I open my lids. I'm inside a corridor. Confused, I swing my neck around and look for Irene and Javen. Javen lies across the hall on his back and Irene is on his right. Both are moving.

I dart my attention around to see where we are and realize we made it to the Capitol building on the floor with Hammond's office and her briefing room. I scramble to my feet, and Irene pushes off the ground and scans the surroundings too. But Javen doesn't get up. My heart leaps into my throat, and I rush to his side.

"Javen," I say and grab his shoulders.

His eyes flutter open. "I have to go to my side," he mumbles. "I need to recharge my Starfire."

"I can give you mine. It healed you the last time."

Javen draws in a shuddering breath. "The Alku maintain and care for the Starfire fields. In return, the crystals fuel us . . . give us the powers to teleport or protect ourselves. But we often have to use them to recharge and I . . . I can't do that on this side of Intersection . . . I must go back."

Tears sting the back of my eyes. I have no idea what is going to happen next. "Please tell your people to come. It's the only way this is going to work." I tap my Connect.

6:14 AM

People should be waking up soon.

"I won't have much time before Hammond discovers I'm here after I make the announcement."

Javen nods. "I'll come for you as . . . as soon as I can."

I bend to press my lips to his. But when I release the kiss, he's gone.

I swing to Irene, who is standing behind me.

"What's going on, Cassi?" she asks.

I stand, grasp Irene's arm and pull her toward the briefing room. "I'm so sorry I involved you. But I can't do this without you."

I stop us at the briefing room door.

"But *what* are we doing?" she asks.

"I'm going to send out an emergency message to all of Primaro, and you're going to hack me into the feed to do it."

CHAPTER 23

"And you think I'm bossy." Irene stiffens. "Cassi, I don't know. This whole thing is stupid."

I look down at her shaking hands.

"And now this!" she continues. "How did that guy—Javen or whatever—get me out of my cell? Hammond is going to catch us, and then what's going happen? Will we be shipped back to Earth with nothing and no way to pay off the debt from getting here? What's going to happen to my aunt and cousins now that Hammond knows I'm involved? They need the currency I'm sending to them."

"Irene, the Earth is doomed if we don't work with the Alku. Like, billions of people will die."

Her mouth slackens as fear sparks in her eyes.

"My father had a plan to use the Starfire to regenerate Earth and still maintain the Alku's side of the Intersection," I press. "Hammond and the World Senate don't want to wait. They want to use the Starfire on Earth for only those deemed worthy. They'll create an Intersection there, but the only people who will pass through are those with enough to pay for the right or who have a skill needed on the other side. We have no idea who that's going to be."

Irene's face pales to a sickly shade. "Why didn't you tell me before?"

"Because I needed to know more first. If there was a way of saving everyone. Now I know there is."

"I doubt my family will be among the chosen," Irene says, her voice thick with anger, and color returns to her cheeks.

"This is why we have to stop the Senate. People need to know what's really happening. Help me do this. I have a recording of Hammond admitting to everything. And then Javen will come and transfer us out of here."

Irene nods, and I grab her arm and pull her toward the briefing room. We burst through the door and look around. This is the same place Hammond made her announcement about mining the Starfire, but it's smaller than it appeared on the video. At the head of the room is a podium atop a small stage with six rows of chairs set up for the audience and reporters. At the rear are several white camera bots for recording any announcements. To the left are five touchscreen computers and control panels for the cameras.

"Can you get us into the system?" I ask Irene.

"I can get into anything. The question is, do we have enough time?" She throws herself into a chair in front of the computers and activates the system. Her fingers fly over a screen as icons pop up. She taps at several and swipes the rest away. A program begins, and it's almost as if Irene goes into a trance while she works.

I turn from her and gaze at the podium as I nervously spin Mom's ring on my finger. I guess that's where I'm going to need to make the announcement. My mind shifts to Javen and nausea begins to swirl in my stomach. Is he okay? I can only hope he's convincing his people to show themselves on this side of the Intersection. It will make a stronger case for what I'll say.

"The system is online," Irene says.

I swivel to her, and the five screens are active. Two are showing security inside the building; two others are wide-angle views of outside for street-level security. It's still early, but as the sun is coming up, people on their way to work are starting to mill on the street. The last system is the computer and screen she's working at hacking into for the broadcast.

"I jammed the Capitol building security. They'll have a hard time getting in here once they realize our plan. I've just about got you in to make the mass announcement. You said you have a video of Hammond on your Connect?"

I look down at my device. "Yeah, it's the last one I took."

"Bring it here. I need to sync it."

I hold my hand out to her and she brings my wrist to the screen. A beep emits from the system and a still from the video shows as a thumbnail on the display.

"That's the one," I say.

"Okay. You take your place and nod to me when you're ready."

I gulp down my heart, now beating fiercely in my throat, and then walk to the set of stairs next to the stage. As I climb, my feet feel like bricks, but I force them up and take my place at the metal podium. I nod to Irene, and the bright room lights snap on, causing me to squint. Ahead of me, the camera bots spring to life and hover above their tripods.

On the largest, a light blinks a countdown.

10 . . . 9 . . . 8 . . .

My heart skips as I know when the bot declares "one" there's no chance of turning back.

3 . . . 2 . . . 1 . . . Live.

I stare into the eye of the camera bot as my hands wring together and words fail to leave my mouth.

"Cassi, speak." I hear a muffled version of Irene's voice in my mind. My thumb and index finger pinch Mom's gold band, and reality returns. I need to do this for her, for Dad. They were brave and stood up for their principles.

"Settlers of Primaro. You may not know me, but my name is Cassiopeia Foster, the daughter of Richard and Isabel Foster. They're the reason you are here today.

"As you already know, there was an explosion on the *Pathfinder* right before passengers were allowed to disembark. President Hammond has released little information concerning this, and I believe it is because she's covering up information that she and the World Senate don't want you to know.

"Arcadia was populated long before Earth came here. It's inhabited by a group of people called the Alku, who live in a second dimension bridged to ours by the Intersection. The Alku use the Starfire for power and transportation between their dimension and the one we live in.

"If we mine this new ore"—I bring out the piece of Starfire around my neck and hold the crystal out to the cameras as one of the smaller bots swoops in to get a closer peek—"the new ore President Hammond spoke of, it'll likely destroy the Alku and their dimension. My father, Richard Foster, was aware of this and had an alternate plan that would benefit Earth as well as the

Alku people, and all without stealing from them. Their leaders agreed to this plan, but Hammond and the World Senate are greedy and want to take the Starfire all for themselves."

I nod to Irene to play the video of Hammond. My heart pounds as I watch the scene play out on the screen—Hammond admitting the destruction of Earth decades before it's expected and how most of Earth's inhabitants will not be saved.

"Cassi?" Irene says in a hushed voice and nods toward the other screens. "I locked this floor down, but security is trying to override it. We need Javen to get us out of here, or we're going to end up dead."

As she says the words my face pops up on her display and I bring my attention down to her picture-in-picture screen where Hammond's video was previously showing. It must be over.

"We must not allow this to happen. I have my father's plans to heal Earth and keep the Alku safe. We can live in peace." I look to Irene. "Cut it."

She taps her screen, and the video bot's light deactivates. She jumps from her seat and glances to the building security cameras. The display shows a large group of officers armed with large rifles. They must be in the Capitol building.

My vision tracks between the other screens where the ground level outside is now bustling with activity. I race over to Irene and take her hand. "I might be able to transport us out of here to the other side of the Intersection. I've completed the journey twice."

I grab her hand and close my eyelids to focus.

Bam!

The sound shakes the room, and my eyelids fly open. On the street-level screen, it's now chaos outside. Security ships are flying through the air and settlers are being rounded up and pushed from the streets.

"Get us out of here, Cassi!" Irene cries as the pounding continues and a blast hits the door.

My breathing speeds up, and I rush us out of the doorway's sightline to give myself a few more seconds. I hunker down with Irene in the corner of the room and close my eyes again. *Take me to Javen,* I think.

Wham!

The door flies open and hits the wall, and the sound of pounding boots hits the floor.

"Please—"

I barely get the words out when someone grabs my shoulders and yanks me to my feet. Soldiers hold Irene and me in place, guns trained on us. The room goes silent save for Irene's soft whimpering.

A pair of boot steps click into the room, and from around the corner, President Hammond appears. She stops in front of me and looks me up and down, then reaches for my neck and grabs my Starfire pendant. With a snap, she rips it from me.

"Take these ladies to the secured cell we've been working on." With those words, she spins on her heels and walks out of the briefing room.

CHAPTER 24

The door to the empty room slams shut behind us. Irene rushes to the small window set in the door and stands on her toes to peer out.

"What are they going to do to us?" she says as she whips my way.

I drop to the cement floor and cover my face with my hands. I have no idea how Hammond is going to deal with us. All I know is that we're not dead yet.

Sighing, I reach to the spot where my Starfire used to rest and an ache fills my heart. An ache for what losing the crystal means—losing everything. Javen, his people, his world—and if Dad is still alive, only Vihann seems to know anything about it. Without the gem, I can't cross the Intersection.

It's more than likely Hammond has now refuted everything I said on the announcement. She's probably making me appear as if I went crazy after losing both my parents and ended up all alone on Arcadia.

Bam! Bam! Bam!

I startle and look up. Irene pounds on the door and yells, "Let us out!"

"It's over, Irene," I mumble, but she doesn't stop.

Bam! Bam! Bam!

She throws her fists to the door again.

"Stop it!" I yell, and she spins my way.

"I have to do something!" Irene's eyes are wide with terror. "Where's that guy Javen? Was this just a sick joke?"

I shake my head. "Javen won't be able to get here without the Starfire and Hammond took it."

She stares at me. "So how did Javen find me at the Detainment Center?"

"We knew the cell you were in."

"So that's it? We're done? Hammond wins, and everyone else loses?"

I shrug. "Except the select few."

A muffled boom thunders outside the building, and I scramble from the floor. "What was that?"

Irene throws her hand onto her hip and narrows her eyes at me. "And how am I supposed to know this when I'm stuck in here?"

Well, at least her attitude has returned.

Several more booms sound. I scan the room as if the walls might give me information. They don't. I race to the window in the door to get a glimpse into the hall, but Irene beats me to it, and I slam into her back. Disappointed, I ease from her.

"What do you see?"

"Nothing," she says. "There were two guards out there before, but now the corridor is empty."

I push her aside to steal a look for myself, and she's right. The hall is empty.

A louder boom rumbles from outside, and this time the building shakes and the lights flicker overhead. I suck in a quick breath.

"We have to get out of here," Irene says and starts pounding on the door again. "Hey!" she shouts.

Biting back tears, I back away. I can't watch her anymore or fear will consume me completely. Instead, I move into the center of the room and sit down. Summoning Javen without my Starfire is just as pointless, but I have to try.

I close my eyes as another explosion shakes the room. With a long breath I place my hands onto the floor and settle my mind, focusing on the experiences I've had with the Starfire. I gasp as the ground under my fingers starts to tremble, and the vibration continues up my arms and into my body. My eyelids shoot open and a cyan glow is filling the room. As if in slow motion, I watch as Irene turns away from the window and takes several steps toward me when, behind her, the door flies open. The cyan disappears as the door slams into the wall.

Irene ducks down.

I scream and scramble backward as soldiers file into the room. But not human soldiers—the Alku.

A faint cyan glow illuminates their bodies. At the exit, several fall back. From the opening a young female Alku shoves her way inside, a female Alku with black hair, bronzed skin, and what appears to be a permanent scowl—Beda.

My eyes widen at the sight of her and I push into the wall.

"Take them both," she says with a growl.

Two soldiers step forward. One grabs Irene and the other reaches down and pulls me to my feet.

"Where's Javen?" I say to Beda as she spins on her heels and exits the room.

She doesn't answer, and the soldiers pull us out of the room and into the hall.

"At least tell us what's going on," I demand.

"Where are you taking us?" Irene says from behind.

But no one answers.

The soldiers, led by Beda, take us out into the street. Damaged buildings crumble all around Primaro and airships dot the sky. More Alku soldiers wait on the street, as well as human guards dressed in World Senate uniforms.

"Cassi!" a male voice calls out, and I swing my head toward the sound.

Max is jogging toward me, followed by Hirata and Cooper.

The soldier who holds me lets go, and I race over to Max. "What's going on?"

"When your broadcast went live, Hirata couldn't live with herself anymore. She transmitted the feed to the World Senate, and the representatives split and declared war. There were military craft at Skybase that came in over the last several days for those siding with us, just in case something like this happened. So, troops were sent in to locate Hammond, but she's gone. The only reason we're holding the other side off is because of the Alku." He looks around. "A group of their people just showed up . . . and apparently the Starfire can be used as a weapon. They took out several of Hammond's ships and have made a protective shield over critical portions of the city."

My chest tenses, knowing that Javen and the Council did not want to use the Starfire this way. I look around. "Do you know where Alina is? Is she safe?"

Max pinches his lips together. "We went back to get her but she was already gone."

I pat my pocket and my stomach drops with the knowledge of what's not there. "I left in such a hurry I must have left my thumb drive with Dad's videos on it with her back in the dorm."

Hirata steps toward me. "We need to get you to safety, Cassi."

"And where is that?" I ask.

"You must go with the Alku," Cooper says and hands me a Connect. I affix it to my wrist. "They've agreed to hide you, protect you. And they will not allow you to stay with us anyway."

"Why not?" I move my attention over to Beda, who's standing about twenty-five feet away with her arms crossed.

"They will not say," Hirata says.

Part of me wants to go with Beda and return to Javen. But Javen's father is nowhere in sight and I fear it's not only the World Senate who has split. Javen may not be where they take me.

"Can you make sure Irene stays safe?" I say to Max.

"I'll do my best, but I'm not sure any of us are safe yet."

I wrap my arms around Max's neck. "Don't get killed either," I whisper in his ear. "You're my best friend here."

Max pulls from me, and his gray eyes swim with emotion. "Cassi—"

"It's time for you to go," Cooper says, and I separate completely from Max.

Tears threaten to fall and never stop as I turn toward Irene. "Go with Max."

She nods and then I race toward Beda.

"I'm ready," I say as I reach her side.

Silently, she raises her hand and smacks her palm on my shoulder. A pulse shudders through me and I gasp and close my lids.

"Sorry that was so rough," Beda says.

I open my lids, and she has a smirk on her face. She's not sorry at all.

"You are not free here," she says. "I've warned my father your link to the Starfire is dangerous . . . unstable." She leans in. "And your bond with my cousin is even more so. I'll be watching you."

She narrows her eyes and leaves me. I sweep my gaze across a small, simple town. But it's like nothing I've ever seen. All the buildings, dwellings, and shops are entirely made of organic materials, though lights shine inside of each one. And a cyan glow emits from every structure. The Starfire? *Everything* the Alku do must be powered and controlled by it.

I crane my head around and stop when I see him. Javen. My heart bursts, lit on fire, heat pulsing through my veins with every beat, and I move without thought as if an unseen force compels me toward him. And I go, throwing my arms around his neck when I reach him. Javen's arms coil around me, too, and I press into his warm chest and finally allow a few tears to fall. I've never felt so glad to see a person again.

"I'm so sorry I couldn't get back to you." His voice is thick with sadness and he wipes away a tear on my cheek. "I had to convince my uncle to go against the Council's wishes to remain neutral. Beda is right. We cannot sit by and allow our people to be destroyed. Using the Starfire as a weapon is a risk. But we must take it."

I open my mouth to speak and stop when, all too quickly, he loosens his grasp and takes one step back. My mouth clamps shut and I gaze up at him. But he's gazing behind me. I turn and see his uncle Wirrin walking in our direction. My heart twitches and my hands tighten at my side as the man with snow white hair and pale skin slows about three feet from us.

"Cassiopeia," he says and reaches into the pocket of his light jacket. "I have a message for you."

He pulls his hand out of his tunic pocket and opens it. On his palm rests a blushing red apple, a Pink Lady, my favorite—*Dad's* favorite.

I look up at Wirrin in confusion.

"Your father, Richard Foster, needs your help. And we may need his."

JENETTA PENNER

Book one of Cassi's journey is at an end, but you can find out what happens next in _Dark Matter_.

Dear Book Lover,

Thank you SO much for your support. I am truly humbled. I would be incredibly grateful if you took the time to <u>leave a review on Amazon</u>. Short or long is JUST fine. Your review will make a big difference and help new readers discover The Starfire Wars.

I would also love it if you joined my book club at <u>JenettaPenner.com</u>. When you do, you will receive a FREE printable Configured YA coloring book, as well as YA book news and information on upcoming releases. You can also follow me on <u>Facebook</u>.

XXOO,
Jenetta Penner

FINAL THANKS

A big thank you goes out to all my readers, family and friends who have supported me on this journey of writing.

Love you all!

Jenetta

BOOKS BY JENETTA PENNER

The Configured Trilogy

Configured

Immersed

Actualized

23030419R00163

Made in the USA
San Bernardino, CA
19 January 2019